WE ARE NOT
THE SAME ANYMORE

stories

CHRIS SOMERVILLE

UQP

First published 2013 by University of Queensland Press
PO Box 6042, St Lucia, Queensland 4067 Australia

www.uqp.com.au

© 2013 Chris Somerville

This book is copyright. Except for private study, research,
criticism or reviews, as permitted under the *Copyright Act*,
no part of this book may be reproduced, stored in a retrieval system,
or transmitted in any form or by any means without prior
written permission. Enquiries should be made to the publisher.

Cover design by Design by Committee
Cover photograph by Jozsef Scheer
Typeset in 12/16 pt Bembo by Post Pre-press Group, Brisbane
Printed in Australia by McPherson's Printing Group

National Library of Australia cataloguing-in-publication data
is available at http://catalogue.nla.gov.au

We Are Not the Same Anymore / Chris Somerville
ISBN: 978 0 7022 4965 5 (pbk)
      978 0 7022 5092 7 (pdf)
      978 0 7022 5093 4 (epub)
      978 0 7022 5094 1 (kindle)

University of Queensland Press uses papers that are natural, renewable and recyclable products made from wood grown in sustainable forests. The logging and manufacturing processes conform to the environmental regulations of the country of origin.

Chris Somerville was born in Launceston, Tasmania, in 1984 and now lives in Queensland. In 2003 he won the State Library of Queensland Young Writers Award and in 2009 he was shortlisted for the Queensland Premier's Literary Award, Emerging Author Category. His short fiction has appeared in numerous literary journals, including *Voiceworks*, *The Lifted Brow*, *Paper Radio*, *Islet* and *Stilts*. He has taught in the creative writing programs at both Griffith University and the University of Queensland.

For my father, Ian David Somerville

Contents

Earthquake	1
Aquarium	6
Snow on the mountain	25
Parachute	43
The Chinese student	60
Trouble	82
Loss	95
Hinterland	97
Room	118
Giraffe	128
Travelling through the air	133
Athletics	145
Sleeping with the light on	159
Drowning man	177
Acknowledgments	*185*

I wish simply to record that right now
life is madly good and please note
this is not at all what I had come to expect.
                                        MARIAN WALLER

Earthquake

He says being in an earthquake is a hard thing to forget. He says other things too: that fluoride in tap water will eventually give you cancer, that he's been bumping into things too often, that he's forgotten the dimensions of his body. The truth is that my father, even as a young man, has never been in the best of health. Before he retired he was convinced that the ventilation in his office was making him sick. He'd come home in the evening accidentally spilling tissues from his jacket like he was afraid he'd lose his way back to work. He was always squinting and biting at his bottom lip with worry.

Now his problem is that his dog has run off. My sister and I drive him down to the print shop to have some flyers made. She really likes the dog. She told me, when we were driving over to my father's place, that the last time she visited he cleaned her windshield. He did such a poor job of it she was blinded by soap streaks as soon as the car faced into the sun. She insisted on driving us to the printer's. I didn't think there was that much need for concern over our father.

Picture both my parents when they were younger. Whenever they walked together my mother was always a few steps in front; my father always followed her, sometimes kicking his shoes by accident, squinting and biting his lip and looking around at everything like he was afraid a bird might swoop him from any direction. This was how they always walked together. I like to think that in his old age he's kind of mellowed out.

In the car park, standing beside the car, my father says, 'Can you believe how many pockets these shorts have?' and I look down at them. They're grey cargo shorts.

'Are they new?' my sister says.

'I didn't notice when I bought them,' he says. 'I've never owned anything with so many pockets, what am I supposed to do with them all? I don't own enough stuff to fill them.'

My sister and I bought the dog for my father after our mother died. It's a dog from the pound, tan coloured and mostly muscle. It has a sharp little tail that whips against everything and my father loves it more than any of his friends and certain family members. It's always been pretty energetic but this is the first time in three years that it's run off.

'You can keep gum in there, Dad,' my sister says. 'Or keys.'

The printer's in a shopping centre down the hill from my father's apartment. There's a teenager on the footpath out front drinking water from a large plastic bottle made for orange juice. As we walk past he pours some of it over his head, then shakes his head around.

'Get a load of that,' my father says.

The flyer my father typed out on his computer has a picture of his dog on it, sitting upright on his sofa. He called the dog Michael, which I have never thought as a good name for a dog, and I feel a bit stupid about it while the girl behind the counter prints the flyers out, and all the time she's seeing over and over at least fifty times, *Missing dog, Michael* along with my father's phone number. He's put down a reward of one hundred dollars, but he thinks that once someone turns up and sees how old he is, he can talk them down to at least half of that.

My father is saying to my sister that some cats will jump out of the windows of high-rise apartments because of boredom. He says he had a friend whose dog hung itself while leashed to a bed frame. There was an elephant on a train once, in the early nineteen hundreds, which was put on a carriage as a spectacle and it managed to break free and jump from the moving train. The elephant had the forethought to do this as the train crossed a river, so it survived. He says that dogs are very perceptive, that they never trust any kind of criminal, that they can tell if earthquakes are coming, or cyclones. We were in another country when the earthquake struck us, but still.

My sister says that he shouldn't be so morbid.

The last thing we need to do is stick the flyers up around the neighbourhood. I'm taping one to a telephone pole and my father winds down his window and calls out to me to put it up higher. I'm not getting it at eye level. We've stopped in front of a community centre and I can hear someone playing a piano. When we drive on to the next place, down near a service station, my father asks me to hand him the sticky tape and a flyer.

'I'm not criticising you,' he says, taking them from me. 'I just think I should be the one doing this from now on.'

He gets out of the car. There's still a large stack of flyers on the back seat beside me. I can see now that we printed far too many – there aren't enough poles around – and I wonder if my father will be hurt if we end up dumping them in a bin. Probably he'll keep them, especially if Michael never comes back. It's bright outside and airless. Cars are both pulling in to the service station and driving out, and my father is struggling with the sticky tape in wild gestures, like a person who's walked into a spiderweb. I'm watching him do this and my sister is watching him too and neither of us is saying or doing anything.

The earthquake came in the middle of the night. We were staying in a cabin in a small town in California. It was the off-season, so most of the other cabins were empty. I don't remember much of it, except waking to the sound of plates rattling and my father calling out for us to stay calm. He made each of us – me, my sister, my mother – stand in a doorway. There were enough leading into the living room for each of us and we all stood there, looking at each other across the room with our hands on the doorframes. My mother looked terrified, but my father looked oddly serene. He had his jaw clenched and was breathing steadily, staring at the light bulb hanging from the ceiling while it swung back and forth.

Aquarium

What had happened was that I had saved a man named George Avery from drowning. He was in his fifties and had grey hair. We'd sat together on the shoreline afterwards, each of us out of breath, but him more so than me. He wasn't in the best of health. The waves had been shaping the sand around our bodies. I'd had water running down my face from my hair and occasionally a drop would find the corner of my mouth. Avery had put his hand on my shoulder and I'd just nodded back at him. My sneakers had been a little way up the beach, towards the softer sand, but my socks, which I'd kicked off closer to the water, were long gone. I regretted this. They were one of the few good pairs I owned.

Avery had called an ambulance from the beach and they'd turned up and checked him out. I had been told to wait around. I hadn't really wanted to make a big deal of things. I had a blanket draped over my shoulders, which I'd worried made me look helpless. A news team had turned up to interview us. I hadn't wanted to be interviewed and in the end I'd told the reporter that anyone else would have done the same thing.

Avery hadn't let me leave until he'd gotten my phone number and embraced me in front of everyone.

The day after this had all hit the news I'd received a lot of phone calls from my friends and family. They'd all congratulated me and told me what a good job I'd done. It'd felt like my birthday and that had made me uneasy. I'd really just been waiting for my ex-wife Violet to call me. I'd been restless. I'd had trouble even reading a magazine.

After a few days of waiting I gave in one morning and called her, while the sun shone big and bright against the white wall of my neighbour's house and reflected into my kitchen. I was thankful that she answered instead of Bill Casey, her lover, because I felt bad for ringing her so frequently.

'Did you see the news the other day?' I said.

'What?' she said.

'Did you see the news the other day? I stopped a man from drowning.'

'Could this maybe wait? I'm trying to get Claudia to eat cereal.' She pronounced 'Claudia' in a stiff tone because she'd never wanted to name her after my grandmother. Mostly we called her Claud. 'You know the mornings are always a hectic time for us.'

'Put Claud on then. So I can tell her what her daddy did.'

'No, I don't want to have to explain to her what drowning is, we're late.'

'It'll only take a minute.'

'Call back later. I can't hold the phone and a spoon while also trying to get Claud to eat cornflakes.'

'But Violet, come on. I saved somebody's life.'

'Good, I'm glad,' Violet said. 'It sounds like a very noble thing to do.'

I considered hanging up on her, but I knew this wouldn't be helpful. Instead I went quiet and looked out of my kitchen window. My neighbour had a vine creeping into his foundations, which I would probably have told him about if I'd known him better. I hadn't been his neighbour for very long.

'I was thinking I might come over,' I said. 'We can celebrate.'

'Not tonight,' my ex-wife said. 'If you're still coming to Claud's birthday we can see you then.'

'Of course.'

'Good. Look I have to go,' Violet said, and hung up before I could say anything else.

I stood with the phone next to my ear, listening to the quiet on the phone line. After I'd left my wife she'd taken up with my friend Bill Casey. I still got on with Bill okay; it seemed us being friends was a hard thing to forget, even if he did things that I'd always found opposite to my own character, like taking wheat supplements instead of paracetamol and using recipes printed on the labels of food cans.

He usually had his eyes half-open when he spoke to you and I had always considered him to be a bit of a moron, but I guess he sure showed me.

I put the phone back in its receiver and went and brushed my teeth, which I do sometimes when I'm agitated. I painted houses for a living. I'd gone to university for about a year and a half, doing design studies, but that hadn't really offered me much and now I painted houses. I'd even started to paint my own house, the one Violet and I had lived in together, and I'd managed to get a pretty good base coat done before I'd left.

When we were married Violet and I hadn't really fought much and some of our friends, both mine and hers, had told us that this was a problem, as it would lead to a lot of unresolved anger. I wasn't so sure about that. The best way I could ever explain it was that we'd lived together for a while and married and had a daughter and then we'd both moved on to something else. For me I just wasn't too clear what that was.

George Avery had been calling my house ever since I'd saved him. At first I just let the calls go to my machine, but he rang pretty frequently and I kept picturing him when we were sitting on the shoreline out of breath.

He'd had these big wet eyes like a sick dog. My house was big enough, but it was close to an airport and when I finally called him back I was sitting on my veranda drinking beer and watching the white undersides of 747s descending and coming so low to my roof that the windows rattled.

When he answered I said my whole name, formally.

'I was hoping you'd call,' he said. 'I took the week off work and I thought I might have called you too much.'

'It's fine, George,' I said.

'I'm glad you think so.'

'It's good to hear that you're okay.'

'Well I'm not sure if I'm completely okay. I wake up every morning and it's like I'm a newborn. Sometimes it feels like I'm learning how to walk again.'

I sipped my beer. It was getting to the dark half of the afternoon. Mosquitoes were out and I tried to shake them off my legs and arms, which didn't do much. My hands were taken up by the beer bottle and the phone.

'Maybe you should talk to someone about that,' I said.

'I'm talking to you about it right now.'

'I mean someone professional.'

'My wife's been saying the same thing. She worries too much. If it's not this then it's the environment or the war or our son being in a different city. There's always something worrying her.'

'Maybe she's right on this one,' I said.

'Yeah,' George Avery said, in a way that meant he didn't agree.

A plane flew overhead and the house shook. The cups rattled in the kitchen. I looked up at its dark shape, the blinking lights on the ends of the wings. Whenever I pictured the total annihilation of my life, I sometimes thought of an aeroplane flying into my house like a dart and wiping me out. George Avery was speaking to me.

'I'm sorry, can you say that again?' I said. 'I'm under a flight path.'

'I was talking about when we can get you over here for dinner. My wife is really itching to meet you,' he said, and then gave me his address, which wasn't too far from my house.

'Soon, soon. I'll have dinner with you soon George,' I said, though I had no intention of ever seeing him again. 'You're definitely in my thoughts.'

'She wants to make you roast lamb,' George Avery said. 'She's looking to give you the royal treatment, don't you worry about that.'

The year Claud was born I would still obsess over some of the men Violet had been with before me. We stayed up in bed one night, listing our previous lovers. I'd been with a few women before her, not many, but one of them had ripped the wipers off my Ford during an argument and Violet and I laughed about that. Then she told me about hers, and we were both about the same number, but then she said that one of them was currently in jail and I didn't find it that funny anymore.

'What for?' I said.

'Assault. He beat up his boss once, in a car park.'

'What?' I said. 'When is he getting out?'

'I'm not sure,' Violet said. 'I guess it wasn't really his boss at the time, because he'd been fired. So he beat him up a couple of days after that. He was waiting for the guy after he got off work.'

I was concerned that Violet was saying this like it wasn't a big deal. She just looked at me and shrugged.

I said, 'How did you even meet him?'

'He was my high-school boyfriend. He was a few years older than me. I don't see why you're worried about it. He was in jail by the time I'd graduated and I haven't seen him since.'

I made a noise, a kind of hum, to try and show Violet that I was okay with it. Then, after she'd fallen asleep, I went into Claud's bedroom and watched her sleeping peacefully in her crib.

Violet had grown up on a farm and I always thought that this had produced a coldness in her, which I occasionally brushed up against. When she was a teenager her daddy would take her out in a helicopter and she killed wild pigs with a shotgun while standing on the landing skids. From all accounts she was a pretty crack shot.

I'd only ever been out to see her folks once.

Still, for a time our life together was a pleasurable one. Most nights in bed we'd go at each other pretty good. Even when things weren't so great, once we hit the bedroom it was like we were both suddenly awake. I'd stroke her body and pull at things and bite them. Violet would be into it too. In these instances I could see how she'd ended up with some of the men she had, as we moved around each other's bodies, like one of us was a planet and the other a sun.

The morning of Claud's birthday I drove over to Violet's house with a goldfish in a clear plastic ice-cream container. The container was filled with water. I tried to drive carefully. The goldfish was bright orange and swam around in circles and sometimes stayed motionless when I took corners. The water shifted around it instead. The man at the pet store had told me it was a female.

I'd made a birthday card for Claud. On the front of it I'd drawn myself down on one knee, holding out the goldfish in the ice-cream container to Claud. She was smiling. I'd drawn in Violet and Bill too, to show that I was okay with things, though I couldn't bring myself to draw them touching each other. They were standing in the background, looking at us and smiling, and

I had maybe slimmed my waistline a bit. Everything else I felt to be accurate.

There were a few cars out in front of the house. I hadn't thought that there'd be other people here. I parked down the street and walked to the house, carrying the goldfish in one hand and the card in the other. Balloons had been tied with ribbon to the letterbox. They weren't helium-filled and they were hanging limply against the letterbox or slid across the ground in the breeze as far as their tethers would allow.

The front door was open. I noticed that the outside of the house had finished being painted and it was a pretty good job, except on the trimmings where, when you came close, you could still make out the brushstrokes. I walked through the TV room to the kitchen, where a couple was standing. I'd never met them before. They were eating olives from a small white bowl on the kitchen counter.

'Hello,' the man said. 'Tony, right?'

'Yes,' I said, stupidly, since my name wasn't Tony.

'There's been a bit of an accident,' the woman said. 'One of the kids knocked the aquarium over in the other room. Violet's in there now cleaning up.'

'Oh. Thank you,' I said.

I headed towards the dining room. Violet was in there, squeezing a mop into its bucket. She was dressed like a cowgirl, with a vest and hat and even a gun holster and pistol. She looked good. There were towels all over the floor, all of them darkened with water.

'Hey,' she said when she saw me. 'You missed all the excitement.'

'Someone knocked over the aquarium?'

'I managed to get all the glass, I think,' she said, looking around the room. 'There's just water everywhere now.'

Around the room were drink glasses and plastic containers and vases with fish in them. Two cognac glasses on the bookcase each held a cherry barb. They were regarding each other through the glass. Claud's lunchbox was on the table and I leaned over to see four zebrafish swimming around inside it.

'I had to put the two catfish in the bath. Claud's upstairs; she's had a bit of a tantrum. Bill's up there with her now. None of the fish died, so that's a plus.'

'I could go and talk to her,' I said.

'Sure, but maybe give them a few minutes,' Violet said. She looked down at the ice-cream container in my hand. 'And also maybe don't give her that yet. Here, I'll go put it in the study until later.'

She took the goldfish from me and walked away. When it had been me and Violet and Claud there hadn't been a study. I went into the kitchen and opened the freezer, took out what I guessed were a couple of frozen hamburgers and threw them up onto the top shelf of the pantry, out of sight. I opened the fridge, took a beer and walked out into the backyard.

There were three women sitting at the outdoor table and a whole bunch of children running around on the lawn. I didn't know anybody there and all the children were wearing costumes. They were dressed mostly as animals, though there was a boy whose costume only extended to a fireman's hat. I sat down at the table with the women and introduced myself as Claud's father. There wasn't any sign of the couple who'd greeted me in the kitchen. After making brief introductions the women went back to their conversation. I drank in small sips. A gazebo had been built in the back corner of the yard. That was new. The pine looked fresh and naked, by which I mean it was un-varnished.

There was a hole in the other corner of the yard. To alert people to its presence, two bright orange witches hats had been placed on either side of it. I thought this gave the hole an official appearance.

'What is that?' I said to the women, nodding at the hole. 'In the corner of the yard?'

'A gazebo,' one of them said without looking.

Before I could explain what I meant, Bill Casey walked out of the house and came over and hit me on the shoulder by way of a greeting. He was quite strong. He was dressed as a cowboy, but it took me a few moments to realise that because he wasn't wearing a hat.

'Hello Bill,' I said.

'I suppose you heard we had a slight incident,' Bill said, 'but I think it's over now.'

'I missed it,' I said.

'It was quite amazing. There was water everywhere. I couldn't believe the tank could actually have that much water inside it. I guess it looks like less when it's in a tank than when it's on a floor.'

I nodded in agreement. Bill had a beard and it suited him. He'd had it ever since we'd first met, at university, and when he smiled he looked warm and familiar. I imagined him having had the beard throughout his whole life, even as a baby. I got up from the table and went and stood with him. I was pretty sure we'd still have been friends with each other even if he hadn't taken up with my wife, though I had to admit that sometimes I found it hard to picture a different life than the one I was already leading.

'Someone finished painting the house at least,' I said.

'And the gazebo's new. After Vi and I built it, other people on our street started putting them in their yards too.'

'It looks like a pretty good job.'

'We were going to call you to help with the painting, but then we didn't think we should bother you with it.'

'It looks good.'

'Maybe we could get some help when we do the inside. The study needs painting.'

Violet came out, with Claud in front of her. Claud's eyes were still red from crying and she was wearing a giraffe mask that had been pushed up on top of her head, so it stared up at the sky. When she saw me she ran over and hugged me around my legs, which I was thankful for. I looked down at the giraffe's face staring back up at me. Claud's blond hair made it look like it had completely white eyes.

'Happy birthday,' I said.

'Thanks Daddy,' she said. 'Lucien knocked over the fish, but none of them died.'

'I heard,' I said.

'Violet mentioned you were on the news,' Bill said.

'He stopped someone from drowning,' Violet said. 'Claud, do you remember me telling you about Daddy on the news?'

Claud said, 'Yeah,' then let go of my legs and ran over to join the other children.

'She's been excited all day,' Violet said.

'What's with the hole in the ground?' I said.

'We're putting in a pond,' Violet said. 'Or at least that's the plan.'

'I need to go out and get a new fish tank,' Bill Casey said. He turned to me, 'You want to come along or are you right here?'

I looked at Claud playing with the other kids, and

Violet going and joining the other women at the table. She and Bill were the only adults dressed in costume.

'I think I'll be fine here,' I said.

'Sure, have another drink. I'll be back in fifteen.'

Deep down I'd always thought that Bill was a better person than me, even if he was a little dumb. When we were in our early twenties we'd come across a dead whale down on the beach. Bill wanted to do something for it. The whale was a dark grey colour and smelled like sea-salt. It wasn't a huge one, but it was still about as big as a small boat and obviously dead. Its eyes were half-open.

'Help me push it back into the water,' Bill said.

'Leave it, it's dead,' I said, but he didn't, and when he'd tried to push it with the full weight of his body from behind its left flipper, his shoes dug into the ground. The whale didn't move an inch. People stopped to watch us.

Bill said to me, and maybe to everyone else too, 'I know it's dead, all right, okay? Jesus, I just want to see if I can move it.'

I sat with my ex-wife and listened to the women talk. It didn't take long before Violet told everyone at the table that I'd recently saved a man from drowning and I closed my eyes and nodded to try to show that it wasn't a big deal. Thankfully the women didn't ask me any questions about it and went back to their conversation about the coming school play and what roles their children had been cast in. I felt a bit out of step and stared off into space.

Eventually Violet said to me, 'You know I helped build that gazebo?'

'Yeah? And you also seem to have a study now?' I said.

'It was your old supply room. We pulled the cabinets out and now the walls look so bare. Did you check out the gazebo?'

'I was telling Bill that it looks like a good job.'

'Did you stand on it? It's sturdy.'

'Not yet.'

Violet stared at me and didn't say anything else. I put down my beer, stood up from the table and went and climbed the gazebo's two stairs. I looked at the roof, which had been made well, with metal joints where the beams met. I bounced up and down on the floor a few times, testing its sturdiness. It was a bright day and the sun was out. I looked over the fence, into both of the neighbours' backyards. I couldn't see any other gazebos. The four women at the table were all watching me.

'Solid, right?' Violet called out.

'Yeah,' I called back.

When I walked back down onto the lawn I decided to take a look at the unfinished pond. It was large and kidney-shaped and I could smell the richness of the soil, like the air before a rainstorm. It was about a metre deep. There was no sign of where the dirt had been ferried off to, there was just the brown dirt of the hole and the green grass of the lawn at its edge.

I wanted to see if I could clear it. I jumped from a standing position – I didn't feel I needed a run-up – and messed up the landing. The toes of my shoes made it to the grass on the other side but my heels landed on nothing and I toppled backwards into the hole. I heard the women at the table go 'Whoa' like they were at a football game. I fit quite snugly into the hole, and I looked straight up at the blue, cloudless sky. For a second down there I found it comforting, I didn't have to think about George Avery or Bill in his cowboy outfit off buying another aquarium.

Eventually Violet came to the edge of the hole, just above my head, and looked down at me. I could see up her cowgirl skirt to her white underwear. Two of the kids were standing beside her. One wearing a wolf mask, the other an elephant.

'What on earth did you do that for?' my ex-wife said.

'I don't know, thought I could make it,' I said.

The dirt at the bottom of the hole was slightly damp, I could feel it on my hands and arms. Violet walked around the other side, down to where my feet were, and leaned over and put her hand out.

'Here,' she said. 'Come get cleaned up.'

★

In the bathroom I washed my face and arms. I had dirt in my hair. Violet was standing beside me, watching me in the mirror. The front of my shirt was dirty. I looked at the two catfish in the bathtub, swimming up and down, black with white speckles. They looked unhurt and happy to roam lazily back and forth in the clear water.

'I found you a towel,' Violet said, placing it beside the sink. 'Are you hurt?'

'My back hurts a little, but I'll live.'

She reached out and touched my shoulder. I ran cold tap water into the cupped palm of my hand.

'Thanks for coming,' Violet said. 'I know you've been having a hard time lately.'

I didn't exactly know what she meant, but I nodded.

'All that business about drowning too, it sounds horrible.'

'It wasn't so bad.'

'Still.'

I thought of George Avery's face, out of breath, his red-rimmed eyes. When I'd first seen him out in the water I'd thought, What kind of an idiot goes into an ocean like that? It had been a cold day and the sky above had been dark with clouds. It had taken me a minute to realise he was in trouble.

'He grabbed on to me when I swam out to him, that man I saved,' I said. 'He looked insane. The waves kept hitting us, getting in our mouths and our eyes. The problem was, after he grabbed me, he started pulling me under so I kicked him as hard as I could. I got him in the stomach and he let go. I really was ready to leave him out there. I've been thinking about that a lot, how I'd made up my mind to do that.'

'It doesn't matter,' Violet said softly. 'You got him back to shore in the end.'

'There was no one else around,' I said. 'Nobody saw us.'

There was a pause and Violet leaned over and kissed me once on the cheek. She said that she'd better be getting back downstairs. I nodded. Right then I could have said to her that I still loved her, even though I knew it was only true for about a second.

After Violet left I wiped at my face with the towel and walked back downstairs. Instead of joining everyone again in the yard I went into the new study. There was a desk in here now, and instead of the cabinets on the walls there were bookcases filled with books. I thought I could still smell the paint cans I used to store in here, but maybe I was glumly imagining it, the way amputees sometimes feel their missing limbs. Claud's goldfish was sitting on the desk, next to a lamp, in its ice-cream tub. Compared to the other fish it looked kind of dull. The lid was sitting underneath the container and I put it back on and carried the goldfish out of the house.

Most of the time when I'm at my worst I'll picture

how I want to die. I've never shared this with anyone, but when it happens I want it to be like in one of those old paintings, where I'm old and white-haired. I'm sitting up in bed and sunlight is coming through the window, illuminating me. The sunlight is supposed to be God, or maybe even heaven, and there are people in the room standing all around me, my family and close friends, and they're looking sad and holding their hands to their faces because they can't bring themselves to stop crying.

Snow on the mountain

Caroline was sitting in the passenger seat while Eliot sat behind the wheel, trying to get the engine to start. She tried not to show it but she was freezing; her hands were pressed between her legs for warmth. She was wearing a scarf and a large coat because she knew the heating in Eliot's car didn't work. The coat had belonged to her ex-boyfriend Tom, but when he moved out he left it behind, sitting in his side of the closet, flanked by empty coat hangers. Caroline liked the way the coat was too big for her. When she stood the sleeves hid her hands.

'It just needs to warm up,' Eliot said. 'Give it a minute.'

Eliot lived with his parents across the street. Caroline had asked to borrow his car because she didn't own one anymore. It was early and there was frost on Eliot's well-kept lawn. She could see their footprints on the frozen blades of grass. Tom had always made a big deal about keeping their own front garden in check and now, in his absence, Caroline had let things go.

'The engine sounds broken,' she said.

'It's fine,' he said. 'It just wants the attention.'

Apart from the sound of the car engine the street was quiet and still. Eliot was eighteen and had bought the car, an old Volvo station wagon, from his uncle. Caroline pressed her hands together tightly, then released them to rub at her nose. The engine coughed and started.

'Okay, my dear,' Eliot said. 'Are you ready to go on our mystical adventure?' He said it in a flat voice and Caroline couldn't tell if he was being serious.

She smiled at him. She was thirty-five and often wondered if Eliot was her closest friend. She'd once mistakenly said this to Tom and he had nodded in a way that had made her feel naive. It had been the same when he'd left her: Tom had presented the information like it was the most simple thing in the world, and that she should have known it was coming all along. Caroline had nodded because she'd felt like she ought to agree, even though she hadn't been completely sure what was happening.

When Tom had left he'd said, casually, 'See you around.'

Eliot drove through the empty streets of West Hobart. In the past Caroline had ordered firewood from an old man and his grandson, both rake thin and surprisingly strong, who would turn up and throw logs to each other as if they were fruit, but this winter she'd wanted to try and save the money. She'd asked to borrow Eliot's car to collect the wood herself. She'd been trying to cut back on expenses. Last winter she and Tom had burned through at least five tonnes of wood, but she felt she could reduce that, at least for a little while. As soon as the temperature began to drop Tom would start angrily pacing around their living room, rubbing at his arms like he'd been attacked. The way she remembered him, he only ever smiled when he was upset. When Eliot had heard Caroline's plan he'd insisted on coming along.

None of the stores they passed were open. Eliot was wearing jeans and a wool jumper and Caroline wondered if he was cold too. He was wearing a bright red woollen hat. Eliot looked at her for a second before turning his attention back to the road.

'My grandmother knitted it for me,' he said.

'It suits you.'

'Did I ever tell you that when I was around four I was with my grandmother in her car. I think we were driving across the bridge and we hit a patch of ice. The car spun around in a complete circle. She never told anyone else in my family about it.'

'Have you told them?' Caroline said.

'No, she swore me to secrecy.'

The tape player in the car was broken and a cassette was stuck inside it. Now and then Eliot pulled at it absent-mindedly when, Caroline liked to imagine, he was deep in thought. It was endearing. She wondered if she would still spend time with Eliot if he didn't live across the street.

It wasn't long before they'd left the city and were in the national park that headed up the mountain. When they didn't talk Caroline felt comfortable, like they were a married couple. It wasn't like her house, where the silence was like someone holding their breath. She wondered if she was in love with Eliot.

'You know,' he said, 'any wood up here is probably going to be damp.'

'That's true,' she said.

'Maybe we should have tried the beach instead. Driftwood burns pretty well, that's all we ever use when we're camping.'

Caroline shrugged, but wasn't sure if her movements were visible under the coat. The road climbed steadily past small trees and rocks. There was snow, she knew, towards the top of the mountain. She'd seen it from her house.

'I brought a thermos of tea,' Eliot said. 'When we pull over I'll pour you some.'

They drove past a lookout and for a second Caroline saw the city and, hanging above it, thick grey clouds before they were obscured by the tree line.

'Am I weird?' Eliot said.

'For bringing a thermos?' she said.

'Maybe. I don't know, like more in general.'

'No,' Caroline said. 'I don't think you are.'

The first time Caroline had met Eliot he'd helped her hang a painting in her living room. Tom had been at work. Eliot had made slight adjustments at the wall while she stood back from it, telling him when it looked straight. After they'd finished with the painting Eliot had looked over the living room and said, 'Now let's move the furniture around,' and once they had, moving the table and chairs and couch, the room had looked larger and better.

Eliot swerved dramatically around a line of four cyclists and into the other lane, even though he didn't have to. He always drove erratically, over the speed limit, taking corners wildly. Even so, Caroline felt safe with him behind the wheel.

'We should stop around here,' he said.

'Let's see the snow first,' she said. 'We can always come back.'

They pulled over into first clearing where Caroline spotted snow. They were close to the top of the mountain. The snow wasn't very thick; rocks and the leaves of small shrubs poked through it. They got out of the car. Outside it was quiet. Eliot opened the car's rear door, leaned inside and pulled out a thermos and two mugs.

'I forgot the milk,' he said.

'Black tea is fine,' she said.

'And I know the lid turns into a cup, but I prefer a mug.'

Caroline was wearing tennis shoes and so was Eliot. When she stood her coat came down to below her knees. Eliot put the two mugs on the bonnet of the car and poured them each a cup of tea. Caroline picked hers up and held it between her hands. Steam curled from it.

'I used to bike ride up here,' Eliot said, looking around. 'When I was younger. I don't know why I stopped.'

Caroline nodded. They were in a clearing about the size of a swimming pool, with a path leading off at the far end of it. The snow on the ground had settled in patches, and a small stream of water was running down beside the road. Eliot put his mug back down on the bonnet and walked into the clearing. He stepped carefully.

'I don't want to disturb it, you know what I mean?' he said. 'Ninjas used to walk across sheafs of rice paper without cracking them, as a test.'

'I didn't know that,' Caroline said. It sometimes worried her to remember how young Eliot was. She leaned against the car. A breeze stirred the trees and it felt cold against her face. She shivered and glanced at the sky. She remembered driving near here with Tom once and anxiously watching clouds coming over the peak of the mountain, thick and grey and carrying snow. They'd had chains in the boot if they needed them. She'd asked Tom to drive more carefully, but he'd told her that they needed to beat the snowstorm and didn't slow down.

'Otherwise we'll be up here all night,' he'd said. 'Can you just let me drive?'

'I just wish you'd take me more seriously,' Caroline had said.

Eliot was at the end of the clearing picking up logs and inspecting them, or flipping them over with the toe of his shoe. Caroline walked over.

'Most of these are too damp to burn,' he said. 'We shouldn't have waited this far into winter to do this.'

'After here we can try somewhere else,' Caroline said.

They walked to the edge of the clearing, but the snow was no thicker. She wanted it to be white everywhere, and deep enough to come up to their knees as they trudged through it. Eliot coughed and she noticed for the first time that he was shivering.

'You're cold,' she said. 'Take my coat.'

'I'll be fine,' he said and crossed his arms. 'You lose most of your heat from your head anyway. I read about it.'

'Do you want to go back to the car?'

'No, but we should walk for a bit.'

They walked out of the clearing and down the path that led away from the road. Caroline followed Eliot's lead and walked through the thin layer of snow carefully, with her arms outstretched a little for balance.

After they'd walked for about a minute Eliot said, 'Look,' and pointed at something with his foot. He had his hands in his pockets.

Just off the path there was a small grey lump. Eliot walked over and Caroline followed, a few steps behind. When she came close enough she saw that it was a dead pigeon, lying facedown in the snow.

'It probably froze to death,' Eliot said. 'They're not supposed to be up this high this time of year.'

'Maybe it got lost,' Caroline said.

'Maybe.'

Eliot took off his hat and held it between his hands. Caroline leaned forward, with her hands on her knees, to look at the bird more closely. There was no blood in the snow or even any misplaced feathers. The pigeon's eyes were closed and peaceful. One wing was splayed out as though it was greeting someone.

'Poor thing,' Caroline said.

'I've heard freezing to death is like going to sleep,' Eliot said. 'Unless I'm thinking of drowning.'

'Maybe they're the same.'

'Yeah,' he said. 'I mean how can they tell anyway?'

Caroline wondered if they should bury it, but then thought it would be a stupid thing to suggest. She considered covering the body with something, leaves or a branch, but decided to leave it as it was. It was starting to snow lightly. A breeze moved like a wave through the leaves above them.

'We should head back in case it really starts to snow,' she said.

'I think it'll be all right,' Eliot said.

Caroline started to head back towards the car when she stepped awkwardly on a round stone which rolled out from underneath her. She fell silently and put her hands up to guard her face. She crumpled to the ground and felt a sharp burn of pain in her left ankle.

'I'm fine,' she said immediately. 'I'm okay.'

'Are you sure?' Eliot said. 'Is your head all right?'

'Yeah,' she said. 'Help me up.'

When she pushed herself off the ground her hand caught in the sharp leaves of a shrub. Eliot helped her stand and propped her up. They were suddenly close and his body was surprisingly smaller that she'd thought. It felt like he could be folded up as easily as paper.

'Try and walk on it,' Eliot said.

She carefully put weight on her left foot and again felt a jolt of pain. She couldn't help but make a noise, a strange kind of gurgle. She felt embarrassed.

'I think it's sprained,' she said quickly.

'Just stay off it for now,' Eliot said.

She hadn't smoked for years but right then,

surrounded by falling snow, she wanted a cigarette. She wanted the smoke to cloud out from her mouth and lift into the air. Eliot smelled like damp wool mixed with basil.

They walked back to the car slowly. Caroline leaning heavily on Eliot. Now and then her foot bumped against the ground or Eliot's leg, and when this happened she tried to stay silent, though she couldn't help inhaling loudly.

'Sorry,' Eliot said, each time.

'For what?' she said.

He didn't say anything else. When they got to the car she leaned against it while Eliot opened the passenger door. She sat down sideways on the seat, so her legs pointed out of the car.

'Let me check it for a second,' he said, leaning down and untying her shoe. He placed it on the passenger side floor and cupped her ankle with his hands.

Caroline was wearing tights and felt Eliot press down lightly on her leg, then again and again in different places

'Does any of this hurt?' he said.

'No,' she said. 'Maybe a little.'

His hands were soft and he moved them carefully, frowning while he worked. Outside it was snowing more; flakes were landing on the windshield, sticking for a moment, and then melting and running down the glass.

'I think it's just a sprain,' he said. 'If you want I can drive you to a doctor.'

'I'll be all right,' she said.

'We should drive down the mountain a bit though. There'll be wood down there that you can actually burn, not all this damp stuff.'

'I should probably stay off my foot,' she said. 'Let's just go back.'

'I'll get the wood, I don't mind,' he said. 'It won't take that long to fill up the boot anyway.'

'Are you sure?'

'What difference does it make? I'm here now anyway.'

Caroline nodded. She was grateful but she also wanted to go home where, instead of a fire, she'd just cover herself with blankets. She'd wear more clothes. She pictured each empty room of her house as if she was photographing it for a real estate advertisement. Each angle trying to hide how unattractive the place was. It made her unhappy. She thought that maybe she should get a cat.

'All right let's go,' she said.

Eliot was still bent down on one knee, holding her ankle. When Caroline swivelled back into the seat, he held her leg for her as she moved. Eliot reached out and, for a second, Caroline thought he was going to stroke the side of her face. He pulled a twig from her hair. It had a small leaf attached to it.

'Thanks,' she said.

Eliot closed her door, grabbed the mugs from the bonnet and got in behind the wheel. He leaned between the seats and put the mugs in the back. The car started on the first go and he turned it around.

When they paused before pulling back on to the road, Caroline reached over and put her hand on Eliot's. She felt the back of his knuckles. He didn't move his hand away immediately, which she had worried about, but instead he looked at her and smiled in a pained kind of way.

'Maybe don't though,' he said.

'Sorry,' she said.

'It's not that I mind, just that I need to concentrate. I almost got hit by a car here once, on my bike. People come down here too fast sometimes.'

'I'm sorry.'

'Stop apologising,' he said. 'You do that way too much.'

They were quiet as they drove back down the mountain. The only sound was the windscreen wipers going back and forth.

Caroline wasn't really paying attention to the road when Eliot let out an 'Oh' in surprise. They were on a straight, flat part of the road and the car felt weightless for a second and then suddenly turned sideways. Caroline reached out and clutched the dashboard with one hand and pushed the other onto the roof above her. She laughed once, one laugh, out of fear. They left the road harder and more suddenly than she expected. She looked down, into her lap. When they'd stopped Caroline looked up and saw that they were wedged into a ditch.

They were quiet for a moment. Eliot looked around himself blankly, as if he'd been woken up and didn't know where he was. 'Is your leg okay?' he said finally.

'Yeah, I think so,' Caroline said.

'There's going to be damage,' he said, trying to start the car. It took him five turns of the ignition. When he pressed on the accelerator there was the sound of the tyres spinning but the car stayed motionless. They were tilted downwards. Eliot's door was up against the side of the mountain.

'Let me get out and check,' he said.

Before Caroline could ask how, Eliot wound down his window and slid himself out. She listened to the sound of him on the roof. There was silence and then the car started to rock. When she looked in the rear-view mirror Caroline saw Eliot perched on the bumper, bouncing the car up and down. He came back and opened his door.

'I think we're stuck,' he said.

'Can I help?' she said.

'I think I can push us out, can you drive?'

Caroline nodded, even though she didn't think she'd be able to. Eliot came around and helped her shift over into the driver's seat. He wasn't so careful with her leg this time around, and Caroline had to bite on her bottom lip to keep from wailing out in pain. She hoped that Eliot didn't notice.

'When you see me nod, put your foot down,' he said. 'Don't stop until you're back up properly on the road. Make sure it's in reverse otherwise you'll flatten me.'

'Okay,' she said.

She started the car then waited. Eliot went around to the front. He looked ridiculous and tiny in front of the hood of the car, like a child at a school crossing. He shouted something and then bent down to lift the car. She wasn't even sure if what he'd said was a word. She put her foot down and the engine kicked in, but the car didn't move an inch. After about twenty seconds she stopped. Eliot was straining against the car, looking like he was about to have a heart attack. He stopped for a moment and looked down at the car.

'Try again,' Eliot said, after he'd composed himself.

It was snowing properly now and the flakes surrounded them. Caroline put her foot down on the accelerator and again they stayed in the same spot. She turned her head to check if the road behind them was clear, and so she wouldn't have to watch Eliot as he exhausted himself. She felt like holding Eliot's hand was the wrong thing to have done, that this had caused them to crash, that she was somehow responsible for everything. The car stalled and she tried to get it started again. The engine sounded like it was choking and then it made no sound at all.

Eliot came and got into the passenger seat. 'I'm not as strong as I thought I was,' he said.

'Another go?'

'Will it even start? There's no point at the moment anyway,' he said, closing his door and making the keys chime in the ignition. Caroline wound her window back up. Eliot was breathing heavily. He pulled his hat off. Snow was hitting the windshield, holding there now instead of just melting away instantly.

Caroline bit down on her bottom lip. She wondered what it would be like to kiss Eliot on the mouth, just once; grab him by the front of his jumper and pull him to her, holding him steady like a kite in a violent wind. She coughed.

'So what should we do?' she said.

'I don't know yet. It's not that late. Let me think of something.'

They stayed quiet. Outside there was the sound of the wind that was whipping the snow around them. The snow wasn't falling heavily, but it looked ceaseless. Caroline was at ease with the idea that they would be stuck on the side of the road and that snow would keep coming and bury the car completely, and that later when people came searching for them, wading through all that powder, she and Eliot would be together and healthy and fine.

Eliot pushed on the hazard lights and they clicked on and off dully.

In the month after Tom had left her Caroline had killed a mouse in her kitchen. She'd heard it moving about each night for a week and had finally decided that she couldn't take the idea of it living with her anymore. She'd bought a mouse trap from the supermarket the next day.

When the trap had gone off she'd been in bed, and she had gotten up, walked to the kitchen and turned on the light. The mouse had been lying beside the trap in the middle of the kitchen floor. Somehow the trap had broken its neck but not actually trapped it. She'd been surprised at how small it was. She had looked at it closely and seen that it was still breathing quickly, and for the first time she'd felt completely and utterly alone. To stop the mouse running off in the night she'd put an empty wastepaper basket over it and gone back to bed.

She heard Eliot shivering and stopped thinking about the dead mouse. He was tensing his jaw to try to stop it from chattering. He had his arms wrapped around himself.

'You're too cold,' she said.

'I'll be okay.'

'You won't. You'll end up with hypothermia.'

The snow was heavier now, and Caroline could no

longer see where the road turned and continued down the hill; after about a hundred metres everything faded into a white-grey mist. Eliot coughed. She reached out and rubbed his back in a slow circle, like she sometimes did to Tom whenever he had a cold. She always felt she was good in emergencies. She always thought she'd have been a good nurse.

'You should take my coat at least.'

'I think we should walk.'

'Really?' Caroline said.

'It'll keep us warm and it's not that far. I can help you walk. It'll be a challenge.'

Caroline looked away from him. His body was shaking slightly and he sounded like he was laughing, tonelessly, under his breath.

'You go ahead without me,' she said. 'I'll be fine. Someone will come along soon.'

'I don't know about that,' he said.

'It'll be too much of a struggle, and we'd go so slowly you'd freeze anyway.'

She could tell he was thinking it over. He always tried, maybe a little too hard, to do the right thing. She took off her coat and handed it to Eliot.

'You should go now,' she said.

He leaned over and kissed her chastely on the mouth. His lips were cold and for a second Caroline hoped that he would push his mouth against hers a little harder, but then he pulled away and the feeling passed.

'I'll bring back some help,' he said, and opened his door.

Caroline watched Eliot stand outside the car, pull on the coat, and then hesitate. He squinted into the wind, looking up the road, towards the top of the mountain, then he hunched his shoulders and started walking in the other direction.

Inside the car there was only the metronome ticking of the hazard lights. She felt like hitting the horn to say goodbye, but then thought that he might think something was wrong and come running back. She held her breath as she watched Eliot continue along the road until he became a dark shape; then, as if he was slowly being erased, he disappeared into the falling snow and was gone.

Parachute

I was playing mahjong with three older women at a Macanese Club dinner and my cousin Chute had wandered off from our table to try to buy some pot. He'd patted my shoulder when he'd stood up, but I hadn't really been paying attention. Chute's grandparents had been born in Macau but I wasn't related to them. I wasn't Macanese at all. I was blond and blue-eyed, with harsh features which, I felt, exaggerated my moods. The three women were speaking to each other in Portuguese and I couldn't follow what they were saying. If I'd been paying attention I would have encouraged Chute not to leave. I was worried that the women were talking about me. I had only ever played mahjong on my computer.

I was wearing a tie I'd borrowed from my father. The dinner was being held in a church hall, a suburb over from Chute's parents' places. They were divorced but their houses were within walking distance of each other. It was one of those modern churches that's hard to distinguish from any other building except for the sign out the front. The women kept talking and arranging their tiles down on the table as neatly as piano keys.

I wanted Chute to come back, even though he could only speak English.

Before the dinner, while we'd stood on the grass out the front of the church, Chute had told me that he'd recently tried to get into the army. He was two years younger than me and had finished high school at the end of last year.

'Don't tell Dad that I tried to join,' he said. 'They're not going to let me in anyway. It turns out I'm colourblind.'

'Really?'

'I can't see red or green, no one ever told me.'

'My grandfather was colourblind,' I said. 'He didn't find out until he was driving and couldn't see a traffic light.'

'When was this?'

'A fair while ago,' I said. 'Maybe in the forties, maybe before then.'

We were smoking my cigarettes. I thought that Chute and I acted the same, but we looked nothing alike. Chute, much like his mother, looked Japanese and had a flat face that resembled a piece of wood worn smooth by water. His eyes were heavy-lidded and he sometimes looked like he wasn't paying attention to anything you said. Our fathers had always been close, and we didn't have any siblings, so we had always been encouraged to treat each other as brothers.

Chute had been given the nickname when he was eleven and had jumped off his roof with a bedsheet, held at the corners, fluttering out uselessly behind him. He'd broken his leg and cracked a couple of ribs. He'd done this a week after his parents had divorced and everyone in our family said that this had something to do with his jumping. I think it was more than that, just like I never think there's a sole reason behind anything.

'Can I tell your dad you're colourblind?' I said.

Chute considered this for a while before saying, 'No.'

I'd given up on the mahjong and so had the other players, or at least I assumed they'd given up. They talked to each other and now and then they'd nod at me. When they did this I tried to smile, but it was a weak smile and I couldn't meet their gaze.

Chute was walking back across the hall between the tables, which were really school desks covered with white tablecloths and placed together in groups of four. He stopped to talk to his grandparents, who were up at the head table. The whole room was arranged like a wedding reception.

I had always been a little jealous of Chute's grandparents. His grandfather owned a chemical company and looked and dressed like a gangster. He let Chute ride dirt bikes in their backyard, or bought him fireworks, and he once let him fire a .22 rifle into a paint can balanced on a tree stump. My own grandparents, all four of them, seemed boring in comparison. I was never allowed to visit Chute's grandparents. I don't think they liked me very much anyway.

Chute walked back over to the table and said, 'Looks like you made a mess of the game.'

'I don't think it was my fault,' I said, looking at the tiles in front of me. I was pissed that Chute was blaming me, even if he was joking. I often had trouble telling that kind of thing.

'It doesn't matter,' he said, and then patted the pocket of his jacket and nodded once with his eyes closed in a way that meant it was time to go.

Chute rolled a joint in his car. He did it with complete care and seriousness. I didn't speak. He lit it, inhaled, then handed it to me.

'It was a good dinner though,' he said, untucking his shirt. 'I don't know what I'd do without them.'

'You had a good time?'

'I think my mother's right when she says this kind of stuff is important.'

'I guess so,' I said.

Now and then Chute had these strange bursts of nationalism. He'd once supported Portugal over Australia during a soccer game and in the resulting argument his father had balled his fists, as though he was about to thump him. Chute had stared back silently for a second, his eyes half-closed, and then told him that it was something he just had to do; it was a feeling he had that couldn't be explained. Sometimes I wanted that feeling.

When we were younger Chute and I used to fight a fair bit. We'd mostly argue and we only ever beat each other up once. Chute had always been shorter than me, but still he landed a few good hits and managed to wind me. I hit him in the face with a stray punch that made his nose bleed. After that we stopped. I was bent over and Chute was holding his bleeding nose with one hand and had the other on my shoulder. Whenever he recounts this to people he makes out like he won the fight, probably because he thinks he did.

After smoking the joint we drove around for a while. Chute being stoned behind the wheel made me feel nervous, but I didn't say anything and he drove carefully enough around the streets near his house. He wanted to get home after his dad had fallen asleep.

'We should go out tonight,' he said. 'Some friends of mine are at this house party.'

'Who?' I said.

'You don't know them.'

We stopped at a red light, near a block of shops where there was a bakery and a Chinese restaurant.

The last time I had gone to a party with Chute I hadn't known anyone and I had drunk a fair bit. Chute had left with some other people but had forgotten me, so I'd had to walk around trying to find a bus stop. He was like that sometimes. I'd ended up walking home. We kept saying that eventually we'd move out of our parents' houses and rent a place together, but he kept putting it off or changing his mind. I had come to accept that it probably wasn't going to happen.

The light changed and we stayed in place. Chute didn't move, he was looking out the window.

'It's green,' I said.

'Tonight my grandfather told me that when they first moved over here they were living in this tiny apartment on the third floor and he would stay up all night with a loaded gun on his lap, watching his car in the street below through the window.'

'Every night?'

'I guess it was a pretty rough neighbourhood. He said he parked his car under a streetlight so he could see it better.'

'When did he sleep?'

Chute shrugged. 'I have no idea.'

I was feeling anxious about sitting in the middle of the road. There were no other cars in sight, but still. I was worried that someone would pull alongside us, get out of their car, and kick our windows in.

'Maybe we should go to your place,' Chute said.

'My parents will still be awake.'

Chute was quiet. I rubbed at my eyes. They were watering. We started moving down the road, then Chute hit the indicator and did a U-turn. We swung around, back the other way. I put my hand on my door to steady myself.

'Forget it,' Chute said. 'Let's just go to mine.'

Driving to Chute's house I wound down my window and let the night air hit me in the face. The sky above was clear and we passed streetlights and mostly dark houses. It had been cold earlier but I wasn't feeling it now. I held my hand out the window and let the air move over it. I was enjoying just admiring my hand. When we came to my uncle's housing complex there were no parking spots anywhere near the front of the house.

'You could park in one of the visitor spaces,' I said.

'They get really annoyed if you're there for more than six hours.'

I was about to say that no one would check, but I didn't. Chute drove quickly out of the complex's car park and stopped by the side of the road, under a tree. When we were out of the car and walking over to Chute's place he stopped all of a sudden and I bumped into him, because I hadn't been paying attention.

'What?' I said.

Chute didn't say anything. In front of us was a dog.

Its head was about the size of a football. It was black and had a short, joyless tail. It was standing completely still, staring straight at us, and making a sound like water beginning to boil.

'Do you know that dog?' I said.

'No,' he said.

'Do you think it's going to do something to us?'

'How would I know?'

Neither of us moved. For a second I wondered how I could get the dog to jump on Chute and not me. Not so he was injured terribly or caught a disease or anything, but I figured he could handle himself if the dog attacked him.

Chute didn't move, though, and the dog was staying unnervingly still. I stepped forward heavily and made a 'Ha!' noise and clapped once with my hands. The dog took a few steps back, then sniffed at the ground, turned and loped back off, leaving us behind.

'Oh thank God,' Chute said, breathing out. 'How did you know to do that?

'It was nothing,' I said.

I didn't want Chute to know how relieved I was at the dog's retreat. I also felt guilty for wanting the dog to maul him. I yawned deeply, which sometimes happened if I felt overwhelmed. I felt petty and glum, as I usually did whenever I suspected that I was the architect of most of my own misery.

★

The inside of Chute's house was dark and quiet and we climbed the stairs to his bedroom as softly as possible. He negotiated his room in the dark and turned on his desk lamp and his computer. He sat down in his desk chair. I sat down on his bed. He owned more movies than books and on his walls were flyers for films, at least a hundred of them.

Chute took more papers from his pocket and rolled another joint. After he'd lit it and passed it to me he hit enter on his keyboard and music started playing through the computer softly. He leaned forward and opened his window. There were several small piles of clothes on the floor and there was a suitcase in the corner, sagging and half-empty. Most of his stuff was at his mother's place.

'That dog,' he said. 'It's pretty dangerous, just wandering around out there. Did you see the size of it?'

'It wasn't wearing a collar,' I said.

'It could probably pop a child's head like an egg.'

I handed the joint back to Chute. I didn't really feel like it anymore. I'd never been much for drugs; usually they had a way of making me feel like everyone was having a better time than me. I pushed myself backwards over the bed until my back was against the wall. His sheets smelled slightly sour, in a not unpleasant way. There was the sound of the toilet flushing, then the bathroom door opening and footsteps padding across the floor.

'My friend Bec wants me to move down south,' Chute said. 'I need a bit more money still, but I'm probably going to do it.'

'Where?'

'Not in this State, that's for sure.'

A moth walked across the bottom of the computer screen. Chute reached out and gently brushed it away. I wondered how much I'd miss him if he actually left; I couldn't picture him bothering to write me a letter or an email or even call me on the phone. Chute smoked the last of the joint and we didn't talk, and when it was done he dropped it into an old Coke can on his desk. I heard it hiss as it extinguished.

'You know we should probably go out and kill it,' Chute said.

'Kill what?'

'The dog. We should get rid of it.'

'That doesn't sound like a good idea,'

'We'd probably be doing the neighbourhood a favour.'

The computer screen was very bright and lit one side of Chute's face. I didn't want to go out into the night and hunt down a dog. I don't know how long I stared blankly at that screen for, but suddenly I was dreaming that I was falling and I jolted awake.

'I'm kind of thirsty,' Chute said.

'Remember when we got into that fight and I busted your nose?' I said.

'You got me pretty good.'

'My hand hurt for a week.'

'Remember I hit you with that rock, though, which was way worse.'

I'd forgotten about that until now, but I remembered the two of us throwing rocks into a hollowed-out tree on a ledge above us like it was a basketball hoop. One of the rocks hit me in the head and made a gash that didn't seem like it was going to stop bleeding. I had looked down at my red, wet hands and been amazed that there was just so much blood inside me. At the time I was pretty convinced he'd clocked me over the head on purpose.

'That was an accident though,' I said.

'Well, then, we're even.'

I looked at the alarm clock beside Chute's bed. It was almost one in the morning. Out through the window the moon had made the car park and the trees a dull, uniform grey. I yawned.

'Oh well,' Chute said. 'I suppose I should drive you home.'

In the car I felt more alert. Streetlights rolled through the car, starting at the hood, illuminating the inside and then vanishing. This happened over and over with a machine-like regularity that made me feel seasick. Chute made a turn in the wrong direction, away from my house.

'Where are we going?' I asked.

'Keep a lookout for that dog.'

'Why?'

'Because if we see it, I'm taking it out,' Chute said, and he reached down underneath his seat and pulled out a small pistol. It looked like the cap gun I used to own as a child.

'You can't be serious,' I said.

'That dog is an accident just waiting to happen.'

Chute laid the gun carefully on his lap and continued to drive. We were driving through the streets around his house. He kept making left turns so that from above we would be making a rectangle box with his house somewhere in the middle. I decided that if I saw the dog I wouldn't say a thing.

'Can I hold the gun a minute?' I said.

'Sure,' Chute said. 'But if we see it I'm the one who shoots it, okay? It has to be put down with one bullet. We don't want it to suffer.'

'I have pretty good aim,' I said. 'I could shoot a dog just as well as you.'

'I don't think so,' Chute said. 'You'd probably mess it up somehow and wing the poor guy. Hit its jaw and not its head or something.'

The gun was still warm from Chute's lap and heavier than I expected. I held it on the flat of my palm. I didn't want to hold it properly, or point it at anything, for fear of firing it by mistake. It looked pretty mundane and harmless.

'Where did you get it from?' I said.

'I borrowed it off my granddad,' Chute said.

'He lent it to you?'

'About a month ago I told him our neighbours were broken into, which isn't true, and he insisted I take it. I don't know, I think it's kind of cool. I've been sleeping with it under my pillow.'

I thought about what would happen if I threw it out the window. Chute would probably get mad, and then I started thinking about a stranger finding it and murdering someone and the two of us going to jail

'Hand it back,' Chute said.

I held the gun out and he returned it to his lap. He kept making lefts. Some houses we passed were dark, others had their lights on. Now and then I looked out for the dog, and at driveways and basketball hoops and the high concreted walls of certain houses. There was no sign of the dog and I was pretty sure we wouldn't see it again, but I didn't want to be the first to give up.

'There,' Chute said, and stopped the car.

'Where?' I said.

Chute didn't answer, he was concentrating on reversing back down the street. We stopped in front of house; a large Queenslander with no lights on inside it. Chute kept the car in the middle of the road.

'I don't see anything,' I said, though I hadn't really looked.

'It's right there,' Chute said.

I looked closely and then saw what Chute was pointing at. There was a brown dog walking on the verge in front of the house with its head down, smelling the grass. It was about half the size of the dog that we'd come across.

'Keep a lookout,' Chute said.

'That's not the same dog,' I said.

Chute didn't take any notice of me, he turned and aimed the gun out the window, with both of his hands. The dog still hadn't noticed us.

'Hey,' I said again. 'Hey, I'm serious. That isn't the same dog.'

'Of course it is. You're just remembering it wrong.'

Before he could squeeze off a round I leaned over and hit the car horn. Twice. It sounded louder than I expected and the dog jumped and ran off behind the house, out of sight. Chute turned back and looked at me. I got ready for him to punch me, or worse.

'Why would you do that?' he said eventually.

'It had a collar on,' I said. 'We've never seen that dog before.'

After a while Chute started driving towards my house. Neither of us spoke. For the first time I started to feel cold. I shivered and wound up my window. We drove down the highway and when we hit the bridge I looked out of the window, down the river, where I could make out the endless black shape of the ocean.

The tyres on the surface of the bridge made a repetitive sound like train tracks.

Eventually Chute turned off the highway and into one of the small streets that dead-ended at the beach. We were nowhere near where I lived. On both sides of the street were low-rise apartment buildings. Their windows were either dark or had their curtains pulled.

'Let's go,' Chute said. 'I want to show you something.'

I couldn't tell how angry he actually was, or what he might actually do to me if we were alone on a beach at night.

The moon was illuminating the white foam of the waves. We walked slowly and awkwardly in the soft sand and then more evenly when it became more firm down near the water. There was the sound of the ocean and also the wind in my ears. Chute pulled the gun from his pocket and fired it once. There was a sharp crack and I jumped. He had fired into the ocean.

'Jesus that gave me a fright,' I said.

Chute fired again. I was anticipating the noise, but it still gave me a start. I looked at the empty beach and the dark shadows of the houses behind us, all in a row down the beach. The ocean was loud. Chute held the gun out to me.

'Do you want a go?' he said.

I took the gun off him hesitantly and held it. I'd

never held a real gun before, but I'd had toys as a kid. I pointed the barrel out at the sea and turned my head away slightly and winced. I fired a shot. The gun recoiled and my hand felt like it was beginning to go numb. I fired again, this time with my eyes open. I couldn't see where the bullet entered the water. I was really doing no damage at all.

About twenty metres down the beach was a sign marking an unleashed area for dogs. It was mostly white and stood out well in the darkness. I lifted the gun and aimed at it with both hands. I closed one eye for accuracy.

'See that sign?' I said, and I fired the gun. The bullet hit the sign, it made a smacking noise and I was pretty sure it left a hole.

'Lucky shot,' Chute said.

I lifted the gun again, exactly the same as I had before. I breathed out slowly as I pulled the trigger. I shot the sign again.

Chute didn't say anything this time.

I lowered the gun. The sky above was filled with stars. I'd heard once that over a quarter of them no longer existed, and that if you followed their light back to the source there'd be nothing there but empty dark space.

Chute was standing a few steps away, his arms crossed over his chest, looking at me. The wind was whipping around us. I pointed the gun at him, straight at his gut. He put both his arms out, to shield himself. He looked worried, and younger than he usually did.

    I closed one eye, the left one. 'Bang,' I said.

The Chinese student

Leonard Beckman was standing in the courtyard that served as a smoking area, near the entrance to the university library. His friend Thomas was standing with him, smoking a cigarette. It was a clear winter morning and Beckman felt tired. His shoulders were slumped. Thomas was bright-eyed and had been up since early, running. They lived in an apartment together, not too far from campus. Beckman was squinting into the sunlight and he thought to himself that he needed sunglasses, then remembered he couldn't afford them. He put a hand across his forehead to shade his eyes.

'Sometimes people ask me what I'm doing and I have to say not much, or I just shrug and avoid answering,' Thomas was saying.

'You have a job and you study.'

'I have a job and I study, but apart from that what else do I do? I spend most of my time either sitting around with you or looking at girls.'

'Looking at girls is okay,' Beckman said.

'Yeah, but I can't really tell people that. I can't say that to my mother when she calls. I've been sleeping with this really tall girl. I think she must have at least half a foot on me. It's great. It feels like a real achievement, but it's not something I can be telling everyone about.'

Beckman nodded. He wasn't really a great student, but he wasn't really a bad one either. Earlier in the week he'd been asked by Professor Blanchard, one of his teachers, to read through and edit another student's thesis. He had half an hour to get through before he met her. She was Chinese and Professor Blanchard had assured Beckman he'd be paid for the work. Each time a Chinese girl walked past he looked at her anxiously.

'I don't think I want to do this.'

'Let me do it,' Thomas said. 'I'll just go up to her and pretend to be you.'

'I've thought of that,' Beckman said. 'But I need the money.'

In Professor Blanchard's office Beckman had tried to sit casually, with his sneakered foot resting on his knee, while the professor sat behind his desk and talked on the telephone. Beckman looked around the office and at the books and loose pieces of paper sitting on the desk in front of him. On the wall was a child's drawing. It had been maybe done by the professor's son or nephew. Beckman was pretty sure it had been drawn by a boy. Professor Blanchard laughed loudly into the phone. He had a deep voice and he usually wore Hawaiian shirts underneath his corduroy jackets. Beckman felt uncomfortable looking at him while he talked on the phone. Through the office door he watched Blanchard's secretary, sitting at her computer, eat from a small tub of yoghurt. He heard the telephone being returned to its cradle.

'The thing is,' Professor Blanchard said, 'try and get whatever payment you can out of her. I'm sure you could eventually get the university to pay you the difference, just I wouldn't be too hopeful about that.'

'How do I do that?' Beckman had asked.

'Try and negotiate. Have you ever done that before?'

Beckman thought of his parents, both of whom he'd always considered easy-going. His mother was a civil servant and his father, before he'd died, had worked for the army writing computer code. His older brother had studied music composition at this university and sometimes Beckman wished that he had musical talent too.

'Not really, no,' he'd said.

Now, in the sun, beside the library, Beckman closed his eyes. He could hear the air moving through the leaves above them. He didn't smoke but Thomas smoked at their place constantly and Beckman didn't mind the smell. Their apartment windows were usually open. Thomas dropped his cigarette butt to the ground and stepped on it. He gave his shoe a quarter turn.

'You better go,' he said. 'You'll be late, you'll be standing her up.'

Thomas bent over to pick up his cigarette and then threw it into a nearby bin. Beckman watched, half-expecting the bin to catch fire.

'See you at home, love,' Thomas said.

Beckman didn't own a watch but he figured he was late. At the café there was a girl just beyond the collection of metal tables, waiting. She had a green enviro bag at her feet. It was obviously her, but still he said, 'Olivia?'

'Hello,' she said.

'Hello.'

They stood for a moment. Beckman had his hands in the pockets of his jacket. He found her attractive, but then he'd expected to find her attractive. Her features were smooth; she looked like she was made from a delicate paper that would crinkle at the slightest touch. He looked away because he felt like he was staring. There was a short line at the café counter.

'Do you want a coffee?' he said.

'Thank you, no. I don't drink it.'

'I'll just get one,' Beckman said, and turned to wait in line. He wondered how old she was. He was twenty-four and had two more classes to do before he graduated, but they could be the same age because he'd taken his time. While he waited for his coffee they stood together in a silence that, to a passer-by, couldn't be mistaken as one between a couple, or even friends. Beckman smiled while biting down on his molars. His coffee was served and he took it from the counter in its weak paper cup and turned to her. He was taller than her by at least a head.

'We should find a seat here?' she said.

'Sure.'

They sat at one of the empty tables in the sun. Olivia took a pair of sunglasses from her bag and put them on. They were black-framed and matched the colour of her hair. The university wasn't very old-looking; it was mostly concrete and had been built in the seventies. Beckman watched a bus pull up across the way, the bus he usually caught, and a group of students line up to board it.

'So you want me to look this over?' he said, nodding towards her green enviro bag.

'Professor Blanchard said your English is perfect,' Olivia said.

'Maybe.'

'He said you've written for magazines and you have perfect English.'

'Well, that's very kind but it's debatable.'

When Beckman had started out at university he'd studied art, but then given it up. He could have told her this, and also that when he was eighteen he'd published a few stories in obscure magazines and once in the newspaper. But recently he'd published nothing and he didn't really feel like going into that.

Instead Beckman said, 'Professor Blanchard's been one of my teachers for a while now. We've known each other for a while, I mean. Of course I can look your work over.'

'I'm not so great at the actual text.'

'You speak English very well.'

'Thank you,' she said.

Beckman smiled. He liked the way she talked. Every word was pronounced correctly, as though she had practised in front of a mirror a hundred times, working her way through the dictionary, but she also extended some syllables, especially towards the end of her sentences.

'I don't mean to sound rude,' Beckman said, 'but Olivia doesn't sound like a very Chinese name.'

'My parents named me Li Wa. I changed it when I moved over here. Olivia was the name that fitted the best,' she said, then reached down and lifted the green bag onto the table.

'Everyone calls me Beckman,' Beckman said. 'Even my mother. I think it makes me sound like an old man.'

'That's funny,' Olivia said.

They paused for a moment. Beckman nodded at the bag on the table. 'So what's this about anyway?'

'Chinese popular culture.'

Beckman nodded again. The bag looked heavy and

filled with more pages than he'd expected. He lifted his paper coffee cup and drank. A cold breeze swept through the tables and rearranged a few strands of her hair.

'I have five hundred dollars left in my budget that I can pay you.'

'That sounds reasonable.'

'I'd have more, but I'm eager to finish up here and I don't want to pay for another semester.'

Beckman put his hand on the bag. They set a date for when he should be finished and he wrote down his phone number and handed it to her. Olivia did the same. He gave her his home number. He didn't have a mobile phone and didn't really like the idea of having one either. He stood, shook Olivia's hand lightly and then lifted the green bag off of the table and walked off, swinging it at his side.

When he returned the apartment was empty. He called Thomas's name once and waited, but there was only silence. He closed the door behind him, put the green bag on the couch, then went into the kitchen to put on a pot of coffee. Beckman thought that he would allow himself to feel worried about the thesis until the coffee started to boil and then he would stop. In the hallway the phone rang and for a second he considered not answering. He picked up the phone.

'How'd it go?' Professor Blanchard said.

'Good,' Beckman said. 'I have it here in a bag, it looks pretty long. How did you know I was home?'

'How much did she offer you?'

'Five hundred.'

'You could have got more.'

'Yeah,' Beckman said. 'I suppose so, but she said she didn't want to pay for another semester here.'

'You shouldn't let her bully you, her father's rich. He pays for her tuition and for her apartment. He owns some kind of company.'

The coffee started to boil. Beckman held the phone against his head with his shoulder and turned the stove off and lifted the pot onto the kitchen counter.

'Five hundred seemed pretty reasonable.'

'Do you know she has a boyfriend?' Professor Blanchard said.

'She didn't mention it.'

'He's rich too.'

Beckman poured coffee into a cup, then took the milk from the fridge and closed the fridge door with his foot. Outside the kitchen window, if he angled his head in the right way, he could see nothing but blue sky and white clouds. The clouds moved along peacefully, undisturbed.

Beckman said, 'Do you really think my English is perfect?'

There was a short pause. 'I figured you could use the money,' Professor Blanchard said.

★

When Thomas returned home Beckman was lying on the couch listening to a record and reading a paperback. He was wearing his father's old reading glasses, which suited his eyes pretty well. He'd found them at his mother's the previous Easter, sitting in a box underneath her house.

'Maybe I should take you out to dinner,' Thomas said. 'To celebrate.'

Beckman shrugged. 'I haven't been paid yet, and I should probably make a move on it soon,' he said.

'You don't need to do it that fast.'

Beckman shrugged again. Although Thomas acted like he never had much money his father paid his rent and gave him an allowance at the start of each week.

'Still, I bought some wine,' Thomas said.

Beckman took off his glasses, folded them and placed them on the coffee table in front of the couch. Thomas was in the kitchen and Beckman looked at him over the back of the couch. Thomas had placed a bottle in a paper bag on the counter. He turned on the light in the kitchen, though it didn't do much. Outside, the sun was orange and setting.

Beckman thought about Olivia, about taking her out to dinner and then sleeping with her. He imagined them living together and flying over to China to meet her family and everyone remarking at how different and tall he looked. He would learn how to speak Mandarin. He imagined buying her mother flowers.

★

The next morning Beckman was shaving in their bathroom. He shook his razor in the sink, which he'd half-filled with hot water. He looked at his jaw in the mirror and ballooned one of his cheeks. He took his shaving brush and started to brush soap onto his face. The sink was about the size of a shoebox.

Thomas was in the bathroom too, in the bath, with the shower curtain pulled so only his head and shoulders were visible. He had his eyes closed like he was deep in thought and Beckman was worried that Thomas was ignoring him. There was just the sound of the razor moving through the water in the sink and the occasional drip coming from the tap in the bath.

'What's her thesis about anyway?' Thomas said finally.

'I read the start of it last night in bed. I think it's about how certain ideals of the Cultural Revolution are still present in lower forms of entertainment. Like trashy novels and sit-coms. I didn't get very far.'

'Is she good-looking?'

'Yes, very.'

'I knew I should have gone instead of you.'

Beckman angled his face in the mirror, then lifted his razor to his face and began to shave slowly. Whenever he shaved he always enjoyed taking his time.

'You'd have lost interest anyway,' Beckman said.

'Probably.'

There was a shifting in the water. Thomas's hair

was wet and pushed back off his face. He took a cigarette from the pack that he'd left sitting in the soap dish. He still had his eyes closed and his movements were surprisingly confident. He'd told Beckman once that when he was in high school he'd been in a lot of plays. Musicals mostly, but other, smaller, productions for his drama class.

'Open that window won't you?' Thomas said.

Beckman leaned over and pushed open the bathroom window. The cigarette smoke that had been hanging in the air like cobwebs was sucked outside. Beckman shook his razor back and forth in the sink again.

'The other day I saw this girl at the supermarket and she was wearing these small shorts and I could see, on the inside of her thigh, she had this tattoo of all these roses,' Thomas said. 'She had these big white thighs, they were big enough to fit a whole bouquet on there.'

'I don't really like tattoos,' Beckman said.

'Me neither, but there was something about it that I found so attractive. Don't you ever get that? You find something so distasteful you end up being aroused by it?'

'Maybe.'

'Sometimes things turn me on, like the smell of paint thinner or something, and I think, What the hell is that all about? Maybe something happened to me as a child.'

'Paint thinner?'

'I was just using that as an example.'

Beckman ran the tap over his razor for a short burst. He angled his face the other way, pushing his thumb against the underside of his chin, like he was trying to gauge perspective.

'One of these days I'm going to buy you an electric razor,' Thomas said.

'I find them too dry,' Beckman said. 'Shaving this way makes my face feel different. It feels cleaner.'

In the lane below there was the sound of a car door closing, and then an engine starting. The bathroom window looked straight out onto the brick wall of the neighbouring apartment, and the upper branches of a birch tree. Sunlight, angled between the buildings, illuminated the wall. Beckman heard the tap coming on in the bathtub. Thomas had been sitting in the bath for over half an hour. Beckman let the water out of the sink.

'You've been in there a while,' he said.

'I've been adding hot water now and then.'

'Still.'

'Okay, well I'm getting out and I need you out of here. Off you go. I have a whole routine I have to go through and you're disturbing it.'

In the living room Beckman sat at their wooden table and started to read. He made a few notes. The ideas were fine, but the writing was all over the place. Some sentences were almost written backwards, others ended abruptly. Beckman looked at the stack of pages next to him. He got up and looked in the fridge. Thomas emerged from the bathroom.

'It's big, isn't it?'

'Only maybe a hundred pages,' Beckman said.

'You're right,' Thomas said. 'I would have lost interest.'

Beckman felt worried about it again and decided he needed to leave the house for a while. He waited for Thomas to get changed and then walked with him to campus. He sat on a bench and read a book. Now and then he got up to drink water from the drinking fountain, then he walked home in the late afternoon. There was a message for him, from Olivia, on his telephone. He listened to the message four times before deleting it, to hear her voice. She'd asked him to call her back.

He spent the next two weeks avoiding her, and listening to the occasional message she left on his answering machine. Over this time he did almost no work on her thesis. He carried it around with him, though not all of it, just the first quarter, in his satchel. Sometimes he took it out, read another section, and wrote on it in red pen. He felt a bit like he was in a dream, in that time would feel slower or faster or would jump ahead suddenly, but all with its own unfaultable logic.

Just before he was about to enter the third week he happened to answer the phone when Olivia called.

'I left messages,' was the first thing she said.

'Oh,' Beckman said. Because of the way she spoke he had trouble telling if she was angry or not. 'My roommate may have erased them. He has a habit of losing my messages.'

'Good. I thought something like this might have happened.'

'Yeah. I bring it up with him all the time, but he's set in his ways.'

Beckman leaned his back against the wall. There was a long silence and he wasn't sure if he should say something reassuring about her work.

'Have you been reading my thesis?' she said.

'Yes,' Beckman said. 'I've been reading your thesis, yes.'

'Will you be done soon?'

'It shouldn't take that much longer at all.'

'Good,' Olivia said. 'This is good news.'

Beckman took a postcard that had been stuck into the door frame beside the phone and tapped it against his teeth. The conversation was making him unwell. He looked at the front of the card, which Thomas's friend had sent from Barcelona. The photo was of some men trying to push a horse up a stairwell.

'Well,' Beckman said eventually. 'You know I should probably get back to work.'

★

To make any real progress Beckman decided that he had to leave the city. If he was at home he would listen to records or read. Now and then he spent hours sketching, because he'd heard that it was something you could forget over time, like an unstretched muscle. When he did draw he drew trees or birds or girls in lead pencil. He needed a holiday.

When he came home one afternoon, after doing what he considered a fair amount of work on Olivia's thesis, Thomas was sitting at the table in their living room, reading the newspaper and wearing Beckman's glasses.

'I wondered where I left those,' Beckman said.

'Are your eyes really this bad?'

'Not my eyes, my father's.'

Beckman dropped his satchel on the couch and went into the kitchen. He filled a glass with tap water and drank it. He'd been arranging Olivia's sentences most of the day and felt like he needed something clear and simple to flow through his brain. He pictured a bright orange rope floating on top of a clear stream.

'Your brother called,' Thomas said. 'He wanted you to call him back.'

'When?'

'As soon as you can, I think. You know what he's like.'

Beckman called Robert back. Thomas sat at the table with his head turned towards Beckman and propped up by one arm, as Robert explained that his boyfriend had left him. Beckman said 'Yeah' a lot, sympathetically, but mostly he just listened. Robert's voice sounded small and a very long way away, and all Beckman could think of was the satellite probe that had been sent into space, to let anything out there know we were here by playing Mozart into a cold, empty universe.

'Can I get a lift to the train station?' Beckman asked Thomas after he had hung up the phone. 'My brother's boyfriend left him.'

'He couldn't have told me that?'

'I don't think he's handling it well.'

'I'd always considered us close,' Thomas said, taking Beckman's father's glasses off and placing them on the table. He rubbed at his right eye.

'I wouldn't take it personally.'

'Maybe I should come with you,' he said, then Beckman frowned and Thomas looked down at the table. 'Actually, forget it. I'll drop you at the station, I just need to put on my shoes.'

It was an hour on the train and then a short trip by ferry to Robert's place. Beckman stood at the back, outside, with his hands in the pockets of his coat, looking at the lights of the city and letting the wind whip around him in a satisfying way.

Robert greeted him at his apartment door. He took

a few steps onto the front landing. He was wearing a shirt, untucked, with the sleeves rolled up and a pair of jeans. He was wearing white socks. He put his arm around Beckman and patted him heavily on his back.

'Don't get your socks dirty,' Beckman said.

'I doubt I'll be the best of company at the moment,' Robert said.

'It's no problem.'

Robert followed Beckman inside. His apartment was small, but not cramped. There was an upright piano instead of a television in the living room. There were books stacked in small piles against the walls. Robert went into the kitchen area and poured himself a whisky. He offered one to Beckman, who nodded, even though he didn't usually drink spirits. He joined Robert in the kitchen.

'Have you eaten? What time is it?' Robert said.

'It's only about five-thirty,' Beckman said.

Robert shook his head. 'Bryan gave me a real fright, that's for sure. I came home and he was gone. I didn't notice anything missing at first. We were supposed to go over to our friends' place for dinner. I called everyone I could think of, so then I had the wonderful experience of calling them back and explaining what had happened. I was distraught though. I almost called the police.'

'It doesn't look like he took much with him,' Beckman said.

'A few clothes,' Robert said, lifting his glass to his bottom lip but not drinking. 'And that bust he has of Edmund Barton. He left everything else he owned except for that. His artwork, his books, his CDs. Can you just imagine him walking down the street lugging that thing? It's solid marble too, it weighs a ton.'

'And he didn't say anything?'

'I found this note stuck to the bathroom mirror. I didn't even find it until about two hours after I got home.'

Robert took the note from his shirt pocket and handed it to Beckman. It had been folded once and was on plain white paper. The note read, in pencil *We are not the same anymore*, and even though Beckman knew the other side was blank, he flipped the paper over to see if there was anything more to the message. He looked at his brother.

'Trust Bryan to be so bloody dramatic,' Robert said.

They ordered takeaway from the Chinese restaurant nearby. They sat on the couch, with their plates on their laps and containers of food on the coffee table in front of them. There was wine in the fridge and Robert said he didn't know how old it was before pouring it into two glasses. After dinner they drank whisky. Beckman didn't really care for the stuff and swallowed it in small mouthfuls. He thought he was drinking how a bird might. Each time he had to suppress the urge to vomit. Robert sat with his socked feet up on the coffee table.

'Bryan will probably come back,' Beckman said.

'We've fought before,' Robert said, 'I mean, who hasn't? But this time it was so wordless. He just left.'

'I'm sure he'll call.'

'You know, I've had other boyfriends, but they were either friends beforehand or friends of friends. Bryan was different. I went out and found him all on my own, and that felt special and I don't think I can explain it any better than that.'

Robert finished his drink and put his glass down next to their stacked plates and the empty food containers. Beckman looked around the room to see if anything other than the bust was missing, but as far as he could tell his brother's apartment was the same. He thought of a drawing class he'd done a few years back where they'd sat at their easels in a loose circle around a girl and been instructed that, instead of drawing the model, they had to draw the space around her body, the white negative that her body cut out of the room.

'I better get to bed,' Robert said. 'I'll get you a blanket.'

Robert collected the glasses and plates and containers and took them into the kitchen. He went into his bedroom and came out with a white towel, a white pillow and a thick white blanket stacked in his arms like a wedding cake. He placed them on the couch next to Beckman.

'Feel free to stay up,' Robert said, walking back to his bedroom. 'I'll see you in the morning.'

Once he heard his brother's bedroom door close Beckman grabbed his towel and went into the bathroom. He stared at himself in the mirror, which was, like the rest of the bathroom, immaculate. The only blemish Beckman could see was the smudge on the mirror where, he assumed, Bryan had stuck his note. Beckman took his thumb and placed it over the smudge. He turned on the tap, waiting for the water to run warm, and when it did he wet his hands and rubbed them over his face.

Beckman woke on the couch to the sound of his brother playing the piano. There was sunlight everywhere in the room but still it was cold and he pulled his blanket up to his shoulders. Robert would play a phrase over and over again, and each time he would try out different notes. If he liked them they stayed in the next run-through, and this way he progressed, slowly.

'What are you doing?' Beckman said eventually.

'It's for an art installation next week. A friend wanted something written for it.'

Beckman rolled onto his back and looked at the ceiling. Robert kept playing. He thought about asking his brother if he was feeling okay, but decided not to interrupt. He briefly regretted, again, that he hadn't studied music. After half an hour Robert stopped playing and went to the kitchen.

'Do you want a coffee?'

'No,' Beckman said. 'Thanks. Can I use your phone?'

'Use the one in the bedroom if you want,' Robert said.

Beckman got up off the couch, still in his t-shirt and boxers, and padded down the hall to the bedroom. He thought about closing the door, but then thought that this would send the wrong message, though he wasn't exactly sure what the right message was. He sat on the edge of Robert's unmade bed, near the pillows, and dialled Olivia's number. He counted out three clear phone rings before she picked up. It was still early in the morning but she sounded awake, like she'd been sitting by the phone and waiting for him to call.

'It's Leonard Beckman,' he said.

'It is good to hear from you,' she said.

There were bookcases in the bedroom, and a chest of drawers. Sitting on one of the shelves were a few matchbox cars that Robert had kept since childhood. The wardrobe in the corner was open, and Beckman could see a line of shirts on hangers and his own reflection in the mirror on the back of the wardrobe door.

'I wanted to call and tell you that I'm away from home at the moment. But I should be finished on your thesis in a week. I'm at my brother's house, his partner has left him.'

'She has died?'

'No, no, sorry,' Beckman said. 'They've just broken up, I meant to say.'

'Oh,' she said. 'I'm sorry to hear that.'

'Yeah, he's not handling it too well.'

Beckman coughed to clear his throat. He could feel his hair sticking up at an odd angle. He felt the coldness of the morning pushing onto his scalp in odd places.

'It's nice of you to visit him,' Olivia said. 'You are a good brother.'

'You know, you have a beautiful way of speaking,' Beckman said.

'Thank you,' Olivia said.

Beckman watched a model airplane that was hanging from the ceiling, in the corner near the window. It was turning clockwise, slowly, in an undetectable breeze.

'I just wanted you to know that you have a wonderful voice.'

Olivia was quiet. Robert started playing again, softly at first, then louder. Beckman looked at his bare feet on the bedroom's carpeted floor. He curled his toes. Robert was playing something different; this was much slower and sadder. The music floated down the hallway. Beckman didn't recognise the song, it wasn't familiar at all, but he could tell that his brother didn't miss a single note.

Trouble

We could hear our neighbours fighting. My wife Karen was watching their house through our bedroom window. It was late and I was sitting up in bed, reading an article about an airline disaster. I'd photocopied it from a magazine at work. On Karen's side of the bed I had piled a stack of essays. I was supposed to be marking them but I didn't really have the heart for it. The fight next door had started with the sound of a glass breaking, and neither of us knew whether it had been dropped or thrown. We couldn't really see much of their house from our bedroom. I told Karen that the neighbours might catch her spying.

'I don't think they even know we exist,' she said.

'They do,' I said. 'It's just that they don't care.'

'So what's the problem?'

Our neighbours were only our neighbours on the weekends. During the week they lived in the city, but I wasn't entirely sure where. We had never really spoken. Usually they fought loudly enough for us to hear them. They had kids, identical twin boys around ten; for a while I thought they only had the one child, until I saw the two of them together. The twins never fought loudly like their parents, but I once watched them carry a television set out of their house, put it on their front lawn and then throw rocks at the screen until it was completely busted in.

'It was probably already broken,' Karen had said when I'd told her about it. The set was still sitting on their lawn.

I went back to the magazine article. Apparently a man had survived because, at the time of the crash, he had been leaning down to tie his shoelaces. Everyone else had been taken by surprise. The article made out like this was a great, hopeful thing, but to be honest, it terrified me. My thumbs had smudged some of the type at the margins. It wasn't printed on very good paper.

Sleeping didn't seem like an option and I felt like a coffee. Karen was still wearing her work clothes. She worked at a café down on the beachfront, next to a newsagent and a post office. I never liked to ask her to make a coffee until she had changed. She turned from the window. She was wearing a black t-shirt and a pair of jeans. She never wore any jewellery.

'I think they've stopped now,' she said.

'Are their lights off?'

'No, but they've quietened down.'

Karen and I had married when we were twenty-two, and I guess we'd been in love, though back then we hadn't had much to compare it to.

We spent most nights at home together. Now and then we went down to the surf club for a beer, but neither of us were big drinkers. We didn't live in a large town and I suppose everyone knew everyone else, though we hadn't made many friends. I'd once heard the neighbours refer to my wife and me as 'the Christians' though we weren't very religious. Karen sometimes talked about how our neighbours probably hadn't gone to university, but she hadn't gone either, so I had trouble seeing her point.

Karen scooped up the assignments and put them carefully on the floor. She took off her jeans and climbed into bed and lay with her head on my chest. She tapped me on the foot with her foot. Three taps. It was a habit of hers that I didn't mind.

'Actually I should have a shower,' she said.

'Your shirt smells like fried eggs,' I said. 'Or maybe your hair.'

She climbed off the bed and went into the bathroom. Our place was small and I could hear it when the water came on and hit the tiled floor of the shower.

Earlier in the week a student had come into my office and told me she'd tried to kill herself. She was vaguely familiar; I think she had turned up to a couple of my classes at the start of the semester. I didn't have a real office; I'd borrowed one from a professor who was on study leave. The girl cried for a few minutes and I sat behind my desk and tried to be consoling, but I didn't really know what to say. She pulled a tissue from her pocket, blew her nose and then coughed a few times. She composed herself.

'You have a lot of books,' she said, looking around at the books that weren't really my books.

'Yeah,' I said.

'Have you read all of them?'

'Pretty much,' I said. 'I may have skimmed a few pages here and there, but I basically know what they're all about.'

The girl nodded. She was quite pretty, not that much younger than me. She had a pair of sunglasses holding her hair back. I tried not to look at her too closely. She stood up, nodded at me once in an official kind of way, and then left. It was getting late. I could hear someone laughing down the hallway, and somewhere nearby there was a vacuum cleaner running. I gathered my things, walked out of the building and climbed into my car. It was a warm night.

I never mentioned the girl to anyone. I didn't really know what to do in that kind of situation. I suppose I could have talked about my father, who shot himself in the end, but all I could think of at the time were my mother's words, on her birthday, after she'd been drinking most of the afternoon. Her voice was distant and mournful and she said that my father had made a real mess of things.

I didn't tell any of this to the girl. I didn't even remember to ask for her name.

Karen came back into the bedroom with a towel wrapped around her. She had a smaller towel wrapped around her head. Her hair was long and thick and hard to get dry. I liked her hair. When she walked over to the dresser to find something to sleep in, a rock came in through the window. It bounced a few times and then came to a standstill on the floor. It wasn't any bigger than a tennis ball.

'God that gave me a fright,' Karen said, though she sounded calm. She was pressing her hand to her chest.

I climbed out of bed and went to the window, but the street was empty and completely quiet, apart from the sound of the ocean in the distance. Most nights you could either hear the waves crashing or the sound of the highway in the opposite direction, depending on the wind. I didn't mind either. I found the sound of the ocean relaxing, and the sound of traffic on the highway reminded me that there were other people awake and doing things. I found it a comfort. The neighbours' house was dark now.

'Can you see anyone?' Karen said.

'No,' I said.

'It's lucky the window was open. Do you think they knew that? Were they trying to break something?'

'I don't know,' I said.

Karen leaned over and picked up the rock. She balanced it in her palm, gauging its weight. I closed the window. Karen put the rock on top of the dresser and put on a singlet and underwear. She got into bed.

'Are you going to go look around?' she said, arranging the bedding around her.

'I wasn't going to,' I said.

'You'd have to find the torch and I don't think it has any batteries in it.'

'I can't see anyone outside,' I said.

Karen shrugged in a way that meant I'd be going outside. For a while we'd had a dog, this tan-coloured mix we'd picked up at the shelter. It was short-furred and sometimes it would bite at us, or stand in the middle of the living room and bark for no reason. Karen adored it. 'Do you think he loves us?' she'd say, looking up at me from the floor where she'd be rolling around with the dog and letting it jump all over her.

The dog vanished from our front garden after a month. Karen was pretty heartbroken. I put up a few signs around the place, but it had gone before we could get a photograph, so it was really more of a description. I wrote *Answers to Max* on the bottom of the flyer, because that's what Karen had named it, though it hadn't been with us long enough to learn this.

We hadn't done so well with the dog, but now Karen wanted a baby, I knew that much. Sometimes in bed she would roll towards me and I'd put my hand on her and try and guess at the emptiness she felt inside her, but still I was hesitant about having a baby. I looked at the rock sitting on the dresser. It was big enough to have done some real damage.

Deep down I think Karen knew I wasn't really cut out for fatherhood. She sometimes said that my own father had done a real number on me. She used that exact phrase. 'A real number.' This felt unfair, but it might have been because I've always had trouble explaining things properly.

I once told her that when I was fifteen I was standing in the bread section of the supermarket with my mother as she picked up and squeezed loaves of bread, testing each one. I couldn't bear to watch this process, so I looked over at my father, who was standing in the fruit section, picking up and squeezing the avocados in the exact same way. I'd thought to myself that it was no wonder they'd ended up married.

My father had let the avocado he was holding fall down his sleeve, then he'd picked up another and done the same, before looking around and walking back over to my mother. I was pretty sure I was the only one who had noticed.

I'd recounted this story about a dozen times, but never in a very satisfying way. My father was prone to these sorts of things; he'd once held me under water with a broom in a swimming pool; he'd yell at people on the street over parking spaces. I could never remember him ever being much of a happy man, and I'd try to explain to Karen how much I enjoyed being puzzled by my father, but I could never really make her see it this way.

I picked my pants up off the bedroom floor. I pulled them on and stepped into my shoes, without socks. 'I think I might look around anyway,' I said.

'Don't be too long,' Karen said.

Apart from our bedroom, our house was dark and I didn't turn on any lights as I moved through the living room and down the hallway towards the front door. Now and then I placed my hand on a bookcase or a doorway to ground myself. Outside it was brighter. The moon was out and a streetlight was shining through the leaves of the tree in our front yard. I was a little on edge, and I clenched my fists in anticipation of being jumped. I made sure to close our front door behind me; I was afraid that if I left it open someone could simply walk on inside.

Standing on our grey front lawn I looked around.

Now that I was out here I wasn't entirely sure what I was supposed to do. The street was empty and I couldn't see a sign of anyone. The right side of our house, where there was a path leading to our backyard, was completely dark.

'Can't sleep?' I heard a man's voice say.

I turned around. One of our other neighbours, David Rutter, was standing near his fence. He was wearing a fishing hat. He and his wife were both retired and whenever we used to have parties I'd always let them know that there might be some noise, as a courtesy. I hadn't done that in a while. I walked over to him. I felt my sneaker come down on the garden hose and I stumbled slightly.

'I thought I'd get some air,' I said.

'It's a clear night. Very beautiful.'

I nodded. I looked up at the sky, the stars. I couldn't really make out David's face because of the dark, but I could see his shape, his slumped shoulders. I guessed that he had his hands in his pockets.

'Did you hear them earlier?' I said.

'Who?'

'The people next to us.'

I pointed over at their dark house. I half-expected to hear them now, or at least see them moving behind their windows. I looked at the short fence between our house and theirs and the bromeliads Karen had planted alongside it. She'd tried growing other things in our front garden but had never had much luck. So far they were the only things she could keep going.

'No,' David said. 'We didn't.'

'They argue a lot.'

'I wouldn't know about that,' David said. He gave a low whistle and I saw Lucy, his golden retriever, come to him. In the moonlight her coat looked white and luminous. 'Good girl, good girl,' David said, bending over to pat her.

'How old is she now?'

'Ten. She's getting old.'

'She seems to be in good health,' I said. Sometimes I saw David and his wife down by the ocean, walking together and holding each other in a way that seemed too intimate to disturb. Usually I'd pretend not to see them. Lucy was always with them, running around in the shallows like a maniac.

'We spoil her, I think.'

'I should be heading inside.'

'It was nice talking, take care of yourself,' David said, in a way that I found strangely final. He whistled again softly and he and Lucy went back inside.

Clouds were gathered over in the distance, above the ocean. They looked like they were headed for us. All of a sudden the feeling that I was being watched came over me and when I went back inside I deadlocked the door behind me.

★

Years ago, when my father and I were driving at dusk on a two-lane highway, he hit a sheep that had wandered out in front of us. The sheep was only a white blur in the headlights, and he swerved, but he still managed to dash its brains across the road. We spun out onto the gravel shoulder beside the highway.

'Are you okay?' he said.

'I'm fine,' I said.

We climbed out of the car and looked around. It was lightly raining. I saw the dark shape of the sheep on the road and had to look away. I've never had the stomach for that sort of thing. The right headlight was cracked and had gone out, but the left still shone on down the highway, making the rain look heavier.

My father pulled the dead sheep to the side of the road and out of the way, even though we hadn't seen another car for at least an hour. He came back and stood beside me, wiping his hands on the front of his jeans.

'Well, that was exciting,' he said.

He was good like that, when he knew what to do.

Karen was still awake when I came back to the bedroom. I took my shoes off, stepped out of my jeans and climbed into bed with her. She shifted over, closer to me, and folded my arm under her head.

'You're cold,' she said.

'I didn't see anybody out there.'

'I didn't think you would.'

'David was in his front yard, walking Lucy.'

'So did he see anything?' Karen asked.

'It didn't come up,' I said. 'But I'm pretty sure he didn't throw a rock through our window.'

She didn't say anything else for a while. I went back to reading about the airline disaster. I was starting to get bored with reading about people dying. I kept thinking that Karen was asleep, but then she'd cough or rub at her nose. I considered telling her about the student who'd tried to kill herself, but I'd probably just mess it up somehow. Karen had a tendency to worry about things. She was always going to the doctor.

'He could have thrown it,' Karen said eventually.

'David?'

'We don't really know him that well. He just happens to live next door to us, that's all.'

'I suppose that's true,' I said, 'but it still seems pretty unlikely.'

The next time my father crashed a car it was more serious. He fell out of the driver's door and bounced around a bit. He ended up coming out of it okay, but the guy he smashed into wasn't so lucky. Afterwards, I'd sometimes catch my father sitting in a dark room and crying, or holding on to the edges of the bookcases in our house as though he was travelling through a rough sea. If you spoke to him directly he'd usually jump like you'd snuck up on him. He had a few stints in hospital, but after he got out for the third time he begged my mother never to send him back. Two weeks later he shot himself, sitting in the passenger seat of her car.

Karen shifted her weight. I could feel every slight movement she made. She was a light sleeper. If there was ever the smallest amount of sand in our bed she'd feel it, and then she'd make us both get up, pull back the sheets, and start hitting at the mattress with her pillow.

Eventually she pushed herself off me and sat with her back against the pillows. There was a damp patch on my shirt where her head had been and she wiped at it.

'Sorry,' she said.

'It'll dry,' I said.

Her knees were up now, under the covers, like snow covered hills. During my life I'd probably done a lot of things the wrong way. I knew that Karen was waiting for me to turn my light out. My mother had died two years before from an aneurism. It got her while she'd been waiting in line at the post office to pay a bill. Just like that. I had a sister who I knew I should call more often. I cleared my throat and didn't move. I thought that it wouldn't be so bad, living inside a plane's black box recorder. It's what they always discovered, sitting in the wreckage, in the forest, in the snow. Safe as always.

Loss

I'm going to try and keep this short. But, okay, there was once this explorer who has, by now, been mostly forgotten by history, and he lived with an indigenous tribe for a while. This was on the west coast of Tasmania, up north I think, near the top corner. The most interesting of his discoveries was this musical ritual that the tribe sometimes performed. What would happen was that one of the men would drag this drum out to the side of a waterhole and the tribe had worked out a way that if you hit the drum the sound travelled over the surface of the water, bounced off the rocks on the other side of the waterhole, then came back. An echo, yeah. So the sound would come back, and then they'd hit it again, letting the sound of the drum and the echo of the drum mix together. They'd have entire patterns memorised. Different patterns had different meanings. They had songs for rain, for sadness, for births. They had a song that was supposed to help you if you were having nightmares. Or if you were sick. Of course there's no real evidence of this; the tribe was wiped out and there wasn't much evidence of anything. Plus some people think the explorer made it all up, because there's never been any proof that the indigenous people even used drums, but I thought you'd find it interesting, while we're standing here, because I don't know if you hate it, but I do, when the plane stops and there's that clicking of seatbelts and everyone stands up in the aisle, but the doors aren't open so we're all just standing around here, sweating and getting angry.

Hinterland

Most mornings I would wake up feeling like I was struggling to inflate a balloon. I was worried that I was grinding my teeth in my sleep. Whenever this happened I would spend a few minutes lying in bed. I couldn't really understand it, but I thought that maybe I wasn't eating right. It was during one of these states of minor panic that I decided to call my father. I'd been planning to for a while, but that morning I woke with the memory of this dream I'd had, or maybe something even less than a dream, some small pebble of memory knocked loose during the night, of him lifting his hand up and hailing a taxi in the rain.

It was coming to the end of the Christmas break and I was about to start my last year at university. I was staying at my grandparents' house in Bundaberg, and when I travelled back to my mother's on the Gold Coast I'd be changing trains in Brisbane. I figured I could see my father then.

It wasn't until later that night that I actually called

my father to talk about it. My grandparents were both early risers and were usually in bed by ten. I hadn't seen my father since he and my mother had divorced several months before. On the phone he sounded rough, like my call had woken him up, then he coughed and his voice became clear. The first thing he did, after I outlined my plan, was to offer me a lift.

'To where?' I said.

'To your mother's,' he said. 'Don't think I can't make the time, because I can.'

I could hear the television in the background and the sound of plates being scraped under a running tap. The tap went off then on again. I didn't know who was rinsing the plates, but I knew it wasn't my father.

'Maybe,' I said.

'We'll have lunch first, then we'll see,' he said.

All the lights in the house were off, except for the one in the hallway that was spilling a rectangle of light through the kitchen door. There were insects outside that would be deafening if you paid enough attention to them. I didn't want to be driven home but I've never managed to win an argument with my father about anything. I'm not sure if this has anything to do with it, but when he was eighteen he'd started selling cars for a living. There's a photo I have of him wearing a tie and a short-sleeved shirt, surrounded by the gleaming hoods and windshields. He was the top salesman every month for years.

'How are Sam and Alice?' my father said, and it took me a moment to figure out that he was talking about my grandparents.

'They're okay.'

'Is your mother seeing anyone?'

'Yeah,' I said, though I suspected he already knew that, since Greg had answered our home telephone a few times when my father had called.

'I really think it's important that we see each other,' my father said. 'I think the drive home will do us both good.'

I said that I agreed.

'Good, great,' my father said. 'Okay then, I'll see you soon,' and he hung up.

Sometimes my father would call my mother, late at night, and she'd always end up putting me on the phone. We'd talk for a bit, but not about much. The only time he'd telephoned specifically to talk to me was when he'd called for my birthday. It was almost dawn and I was still in bed, half-asleep.

'I wanted to be the first to wish you a happy birthday,' he said. 'Am I the first? You haven't spoken to anyone else yet, have you?'

'No,' I said. 'I haven't.'

Outside it was starting to get light and I could hear the calls of birds and it made my head feel empty.

★

My father was waiting for me on the street out in front of the train station. The city was hot and I was wearing jeans and a t-shirt and I could already feel sweat running down my back. My father had a newspaper tucked under his arm and he was wearing a light grey suit with no tie. It was good to see him. He hugged me, thumped me twice on the back in greeting, and took my bag off me.

'It's been too long,' he said. 'I was going to get you a present of some sort, but I didn't know what to get you. I went into a toy store, to buy you something as a joke, but then I thought it probably wouldn't be that funny. I'll buy you lunch, though. And maybe something else.'

'It's okay, Dad' I said.

'Hurry it up,' he said. 'I'm parked in that bus stop over there.'

We walked over to his car and my father threw my bag on the back seat, which was mostly taken up by a bag of golf clubs and a golfing umbrella. The car was shiny and black and looked new.

'I bought a whole bunch of golf balls on sale,' he said. 'I've been driving to the river at night and smacking them into the water with a nine iron. There's a certain kind of therapy in it.'

I nodded and didn't say anything.

'Do you like this car? It's new, I just got it.'

'It's pretty nice,' I said.

'Touch the roof,' he said.

I hesitated, then reached out and touched the roof of the car.

'I had it waxed. The whole car's like a big black slippery rock.'

I smiled and tried to seem enthusiastic, then went and sat in the passenger seat. My father climbed in behind the wheel. Up close I noticed that he hadn't shaved in a while and that his suit looked like he'd been wearing it for a couple of days. He smelled faintly of liquorice, and underneath his eyes were dark smudges. He spat out his open window and pulled out onto the street.

'I'm not used to this car yet,' he said. 'The indicator's on the opposite side to my old car, and for some reason this means I occasionally make left turns when I want to go right. It's mixed my brain around or something.'

To illustrate his point he swerved the car back and forth.

'That sounds pretty dangerous,' I said.

'It's not as serious as you'd think,' he said.

We briefly drove through the city, now and then waiting at traffic lights and looking for a parking space on the street, until my father gave up and parked under a shopping centre. We climbed out of the car. It felt airless down here. Whenever cars turned the corners of the car park their tyres whined on the concrete.

'Can you believe I've never had a car that's had automatic locking before? Do you want to press it?'

'Press what?' I said.

'Do you want to press the button that locks the car?'

'No thanks,' I said. 'I'm not a child.'

My father shrugged and said, 'I thought you'd get a kick out of it.'

I wasn't sure if he was messing with me. The car made a whistling noise and its indicators blinked. We walked up a staircase to street level and my father headed down the street immediately. I followed him, only a few steps behind.

'Where are we going?' I said to the back of his head.

'A bar that I go to sometimes,' he said. 'I think you'll like it, it's quiet and it's dark.'

My parents hadn't fought that much while they were married; they were more like two people politely talking to each other on a bus. Maybe it would have been easier for me if there was more to get angry at, but it was more casual than that. I started stealing things after my father left. I took small things that I didn't really need, like batteries and toothbrushes. I did this for a few weeks and then I gave it up, I think because no one really noticed.

The bar we were headed for was down a flight of stairs. It was under a store that sold discounted books. There were booths along the sides of the room and barrels as tables, with bar stools around them, over near the bar. My father nodded towards a booth, meaning for me to sit down, and ordered two pints of beer. It was almost three in the afternoon. There weren't many people in the bar.

'I have to get a train before six,' I said when my father sat down across from me. 'That way I can still catch the bus home.'

'Listen, I'll drive you home and that's that,' my father said.

'I don't want to put you out.'

'No. It's no trouble.'

I drank my beer. There was a soccer game playing on a television above the bar, but the sound was muted. My father drank too. There were three loud men sitting around one of the barrels. All three of them looked like businessmen, but had dumped their jackets and ties.

'I know it's been a while but you're looking good,' my father said. 'When you were younger I always worried that you had too shapely hips, but I guess you turned out all right.'

'What?' I said.

'It was just an observation, there's no need to get offended about it.'

'I'm not offended,' I said.

My father was already halfway through his drink. I said that I needed to go to the bathroom and I got up. He nodded and held up his hand. I walked across the empty dance floor and scratched at the back of my head, which is something I do when I feel like I'm being observed. The bathroom smelled of soap made from citric acid and there was a cockroach lying dead on its back near the drain of the urinal. I wondered if I could get out of the bar without my father noticing. Our booth had a clear view of the staircase we'd entered by, but even if I did manage to escape he'd probably still track me down at the train station.

When I came out of the bathroom my father wasn't alone. There was a woman sitting next to him, tipping her head back to drain her glass. She brought the glass back down to the table. It had a lemon wedge stuck in the bottom of it and a few ice cubes. There was a black straw discarded on the table. I guessed that the woman was at least ten years younger than my father. I sat down across from them but didn't say anything. The woman had thick blond hair and earrings that were large and looked like they were made from varnished wood. She was chewing on an ice cube. It made my teeth ache.

'Here he is,' my father said to her; then to me, 'Evan, this is Patricia.'

'Hi,' she said, after swallowing.

'Evan here is an engineering student. He just built a dam, an entire dam. He designed the whole thing himself.'

'That's pretty amazing,' Patricia said. 'You seem too young to have done that.'

'It was for a company I was doing work experience with,' I said, surprised how impressed my father sounded. 'It's not very big.'

Earlier in the year I had built a dam on a river out in the hinterland, not too far from where I was living with my mother and Greg. Before construction began I had gone to the site and walked up and down the river. It was a hot afternoon and there was no one around. I didn't see any animals either. At certain points the river became so thin it could be easily jumped over, but it flowed steadily and I had sat by it for a while, throwing sticks into the water and watching them float downstream. For about a week I went over the plans looking for faults until I had to force myself to quit worrying about it. Next thing I knew I was waking in a panic, though I still wasn't entirely convinced this was on account of the dam.

'Do you two know each other?' I said.

'Not yet,' Patricia said.

My father fished the wedge of lemon from Patricia's empty glass. He sucked the pulp off it then dropped it onto the table. We all looked at it for a moment. It looked like a broken yellow boat. I finished my drink.

'Do you want another one?' my father said.

'We should probably go.'

'We just got here, we don't need to go just yet.'

'Where are you going?' Patricia said.

Patricia's hands were under the table, and I figured it would be strange if I asked to see them. My father leaned back into the booth. He looked at me in the same way he did when I was younger and he used to beat me at chess.

'I'm dropping the kid here off at his mother's.'

'And we're late,' I said.

'We're not late, you don't have to be there at any set time,' my father said. He turned to Patricia. 'He always used to get like this when he was a kid. You should've seen the panic on his face if we were ever late for the movies. He used to look like he was ill.'

'We were always late for movies,' I said. 'We always missed the start.'

'Not always,' my father said. 'Usually just the trailers.'

Patricia looked at the table and flicked one end of the lemon wedge so it spun on the spot. Her nails were painted a shade of pink that was barely noticeable unless they caught the light.

'Hey look, maybe you should come with us,' my father said. 'It only takes about an hour or so to drive there.'

Patricia looked at me and I tried to smile, but I'm sure it was obvious that I was biting my tongue. My father had a habit of inviting strangers to spend time with us. He once brought a young couple into our house on Christmas morning. They had been trying to find a way down to the beach. My father had offered them a drink, which they politely declined, but he insisted on it and made a big fuss until they were standing with us in our living room, each with a glass of champagne.

'I'll be all right,' Patricia said. 'You two go have your fun.'

We walked back towards the car. It was getting late in the afternoon but the sun was still hot and white between the buildings. The sky was bright blue. My father walked beside me this time, at the same pace.

'I'm glad that woman's not coming with us,' he said. 'I don't think it would have worked out. It would have been a pretty awkward ride down there.'

'I thought you were seeing someone,' I said.

'Is that what your mother said? Maybe, I don't know. I don't need to discuss this kind of thing with you.'

'What would you have done if Patricia had wanted to come with us?'

My father stopped walking and considered the question. People walked around us. I tried to keep out of the way.

'I suppose I hadn't really thought about that,' he said. 'We could have ditched her on the street probably.'

To get to the car park we walked into the shopping centre and down a concrete stairwell. My father unlocked the car as soon at it was in sight, raising his keychain like he was firing a gun. Before we drove off we sat with the engine on and the air conditioner on high.

'I need to cool down before I drive,' my father said. 'I can't even think about driving this thing until that happens.'

A car stopped in front of us in the car park, waiting for us to pull out of our space. My father looked at the car for a long time, then he put his car in gear and followed the exit signs out onto the street.

We drove south with the sun making its slow decline behind the western hills. My father didn't talk much, or have the radio on, and we sat in a silence that was only interrupted by the steady clicking of the indicator when we changed lanes. Sometimes the car would drift a little and hit the audible lines on the side of the road. Whenever this happened my father would swerve the car suddenly, as if burned, and straighten our course. I would have tried to get some sleep, because I felt hot and exhausted, but there was a fair chance I'd wake up shouting or in a panicked sweat and I didn't need my father seeing that.

By the time we turned off the highway the sun was out of sight. We followed a road past a service station and empty green fields. I watched a flock of white birds flying in a loose formation. My mother had moved out of the city and into the hinterland a month after my father left, to an acreage of dirt and rocks and trees and a house with three small bedrooms. There was an above-ground swimming pool in the backyard filled mostly with rainwater. There was usually a layer of leaves and eucalyptus oil on the surface of the water.

'Are we almost there?' my father said after a while.

'I think so,' I said, looking around. The road we were on looked unfamiliar. 'Just keep going, I'm sure it's this way.'

'You're sure.'

I nodded. There was a river beside us that I thought I'd seen before. The sky was a deep blue. My father put his headlights on.

'Do you remember when we were driving in that national park and we saw that car off the road and upside down and I stopped to see if anyone was inside?' he said.

'Yeah,' I said.

'I know it turned out to be empty, but that was a terrifying thing to do. I hated doing that.'

What I remembered was standing on the side of the road and looking down a bank at the car, which had been stopped from sliding further down the hill by trees. My father told me to stay where I was and climbed down to see if anyone was hurt. It looked like a suitcase had exploded. I didn't like seeing the clothes on the ground everywhere.

★

It was getting dark and the surface of the road had turned to gravel. The car shook and I could hear individual rocks hitting the bottom of the car, thrown up by the tyres. I looked around but there was just the occasional driveway and trees and not much else.

'I don't know where we are,' I said.

'What?' my father said.

'I thought I did, but we must have taken a wrong turn somewhere.'

'You couldn't have said something earlier?'

'I know,' I said. 'I should have.'

My father shook his head. He didn't slow down, instead he kept on driving down the road, following our headlights that were starting to push through the darkness.

'We'll keep going until we see a sign, then we can try to get our bearings,' my father said. 'Have you noticed that some of these driveways are as wide as roads?'

'Yeah,' I said.

'It's very disorientating.'

We came to a T-junction and my father slowed down; there were no signs. On the right of us there was a barbed-wire fence and on the left an empty field. Ahead of us were trees. My father stopped the car. He looked around, peering over the steering wheel in what I felt was an exaggerated way. He was acting as though he was losing his eyesight.

'There's no signs. How do they expect us to get out of here?' he said.

'Maybe we should just go back,' I said.

'To where? You obviously have no idea where we are.'

I didn't say anything. The dust that our car had thrown up off the road floated and turned in the headlights. I started to imagine that the dust was coming through the air conditioner and blowing into my face and I had to clear my throat from the thought of it.

'Maybe the sign's fallen over,' I said. 'It could be right there.'

'So go check,' he said.

I got out of the car and walked across the road. I kicked a large stone on the road with the toe of my sneaker and looked around. There wasn't anything in sight. Heading back to the car I raised my hand up to shield my eyes from the headlights.

'Nothing,' I said.

'We'll go back to that service station, ask directions,' my father said, turning the car around and heading back down the road.

'I'm sorry,' I said.

He drove faster. The road was empty and above us stars were starting to appear as the dark blue sky faded to black. I put my foot up on the glove box, then took it down again. I'd left a shoe print in light brown dust and I wiped at it with my hand.

'I know your mother's living with someone now,' my father said, 'and I'm still adjusting to the idea of meeting him. I don't need to tell you I've been nervous about the whole thing. Sometimes I plan it out in my head and I'm civil and we joke around, then other times all I want to do is punch his face in.'

'He's away for a fortnight,' I said. 'At a business retreat.'

My father looked at me for a second before turning his attention back to the road. 'Well, it'll be good to see your mother anyway.'

The service station had four petrol pumps. There was a sign with a silhouette of a whale on it in bright red paint. My father stopped in the car park.

'Wait here and I'll go ask,' he said. 'You know, before, when you got out of the car, I thought about driving off and leaving you. I didn't, though, and I'm feeling much better about the whole situation now.'

He closed the car door and walked inside the service station, adjusting the collar on his suit. I could see him through the window, talking to the guy behind the counter. My father was leaning forward with both his elbows on the counter. I got out of the car and saw that I had five missed calls from my mother. I called her back.

'Hey it's me,' I said, when she picked up.

'Evan? Where are you?' my mother said. 'I thought you'd be here hours ago, what happened? Is everything okay?'

I could see the man behind the counter saying something and my father starting to laugh this big fake laugh. Even from outside I could see that. The guy probably could tell that he was faking it too, and for a second I felt sorry for my father. The guy said something else and my father laughed again.

'I'm all right,' I said to my mother. 'Dad decided to drive me home. I'll see you soon.'

'What?' my mother said and I hung up and turned off my phone. I walked into the service station.

On the counter my father was writing down directions in the margin of a newspaper, which he then tore off, and thanked the guy by shaking his hand. When he turned to leave he saw me and frowned.

'I thought you were waiting in the car,' he said, walking over to me. 'Did you want me to buy you something?'

'No,' I said.

The fluorescent lights made him look sickly and much older than he was. I walked over and grabbed a chocolate bar from one of the aisles, below a stack of magazines. I slipped it into my pocket. My father looked at me and I looked back, and I tried to nod at him in a confident way, to let him know I could handle this. I headed towards the door and walked out into the warm night air, my father a few steps behind me.

'Are you taking that?' he said.

I didn't reply. There were bugs orbiting the lights above the pumps. It was quiet enough to hear the hum of cars on the highway, which, I realised then, probably wasn't that far away. I walked over to the car, opened the door and got in. I forced myself not to turn around and look back. My father got into the car and looked at me for a short time before starting the engine. He pulled out of the car park and onto the road.

'I have proper directions now,' he said. 'So I know where we're going.'

The drive seemed slower now that my father had directions and I didn't have to look anxiously at the blank trees, illuminated by the headlights, passing us by on the side of the road. When we slowed and turned into my mother's driveway my father said, 'This is it?' in a dissatisfied way.

'Yeah,' I said.

Our house was in a clearing cut out of the bush. It had corrugated-iron sides and, I noticed, looking at it now, resembled a shed. Inside were hardwood floors that had been laid over concrete. All the lights in the house were turned on. My father drove around the side of the house and parked in the backyard, beside the swimming pool.

'Let me give you some money,' he said, taking his wallet from the inside pocket of his jacket.

'What?' I said.

'Instead of a present. So you can go get yourself something.'

He held out a fifty-dollar note and I stared at it for a second before taking it and pushing it into my pocket.

'Just be sure to tell me what you bought, the next time we speak on the phone.'

My mother was standing at the sliding door at the side of the house. She raised her hand. My father got out of the car and I followed. The air smelled richly of eucalyptus. I followed a few steps behind my father. The packed-dirt driveway ran all the way up to the door where my mother was standing.

'Hello, Teresa,' my father said.

My mother nodded once with her back straightened. A look of concern moved across the surface of her face. She smiled.

'Hello,' she said. 'Evan said you were coming.'

My father looked at me, then at the house. He took in the walls and the roof and then insides of the house, as much as he could see past my mother in the doorway.

'This place isn't bad, is it?' he said.

'Come inside,' my mother said. 'You must be exhausted.'

'One minute.'

My mother put her arm around me and kissed me on the cheek, then we both watched my father walk around the side of the house. With his hand he tested the strength of the piping that ran from the gutter on the roof to the large concrete tank beside the house. Once he was satisfied that it was secure, he walked over and looked into the dark water of the swimming pool.

'The pool could use a clean,' he said. 'I wouldn't want to swim in that.'

'We rarely use it at the moment,' my mother said.

'You just need to clean it once, then it's easy to maintain. Your boyfriend should know that. Where's your pool cover?'

My mother shrugged and walked inside and my father and I followed. There was a pot of soup on the stove and dishes piled in the kitchen sink. My mother's dressing-gown was lying on the couch. Usually, at this time of the night, she'd be wearing it, but instead she was dressed in a wool skirt and shirt. She'd also tied her hair back.

'You look nice,' my father said.

'Thank you,' my mother said.

She had her arms crossed and my father reached out and gently touched her elbow, once. He cleared his throat and then he looked over at me.

'Evan, do you mind getting your bag?' he said.

I walked out into the night and opened the door to the back seat of the car. The light inside the car came on. I put my bag over my shoulder and it made me feel off balance. I wasn't used to its weight.

Inside, in the warm glow of the kitchen, my father

was talking quietly to my mother. She was looking at the floor and nodding. They both looked very serious. My father was talking very quickly and holding my mother's elbow again. I picked up the umbrella from the back seat, closed the door, then scraped it across all the pretty black paint on the side of my father's car. The noise made me wince. I could hear the side door opening. I scraped another line, this time heading back in the other direction. The sound was worse. I ignored it.

Room

Room 805 was an average-looking room. One double bed, a desk, a chair, a thick shelf with a radio built into it like the dashboard of a car. Unlike the hallway outside, where the carpet was a deep red, the floor inside the room was a sickly off-white. The lamp beside the desk was the only light in the room that was turned on. At first this had been a problem, but it helped set the mood. There was a sliding glass door that led out to a small balcony. He had been instructed to keep this door closed at all times. Outside there were the lights of the surrounding office buildings and numbers, lit up in yellow, on the face of a large digital clock on the roof of a skyscraper. Down in the street were the taillights of cars and also a church, the orange spotlights around it making the sandstone brick walls glow. He tapped his fingers on the desk, in time with a tune only he could hear.

She came up at seven, holding a purse. He told her he'd only been waiting for ten minutes, but really he'd been there for half the day preparing. He'd taken off his shoes and they were sitting together neatly at the foot of the bed.

'Maybe some music?' she said.

'You can try the radio,' he said. 'But I'm pretty sure it's busted.'

The wiring in the radio had been tampered with earlier so there would be no other sounds in the room apart from their voices. He looked nervous, but talking seemed to help calm the quiver in his voice. Now and then he'd rub at his right eye. He coughed once into his fist while they stood there looking at each other.

'I'd love a drink,' she said.

'I ordered a bottle, it's on its way up.'

He cast a quick glance at the mirror on the wall opposite the bed, which he'd been told to try to avoid. She put her purse down on the bed. She was pretty and wearing a dress that looked new. It showed off her figure. She was wearing make-up, but not too much.

I had never seen the dress before. The image of her standing there beside the bed was caught and broken down into millions of tiny squares and sent through an optical cable and placed back in order onto the monitor that was sitting in front of me. For a second the image spiked and I adjusted the connection by hitting the side of the monitor. I had been following her for months, mainly just watching her through the zoom lens of a camera pointed through the wound-down window of my car and listening to her voice through a tap in her phone line. She only ever called the members of her family. Her mother was sick. Her sister was there with them but her father wasn't coping well; he'd let the plants die. She didn't have many friends.

She worked as an administrative assistant in a law firm in the city. She went to yoga classes every Thursday night. Did most of her shopping at a health food store a couple of streets away from her house. In her fridge she had leftover meals in containers, their contents marked by masking tape, bitten at and torn rather than cut with scissors, and written on in black felt-tip pen. As far as I could tell her only vices were store-bought orange juice (neither low fat nor low GI) and a half-empty bottle of vodka in the freezer. There was also a packet of cigarettes in one of the drawers, but this seemed to be for sentimental reasons more than anything else. Not once had I seen her light one.

It was a relief to see her in the dress, showing off her figure, because I was worried that she had been apprehensive about the whole encounter.

There was a knock at the door and I adjusted my headphones and toyed with the sound levels to smooth out a small patch of distortion. I had installed three cameras in the main room – one directly behind the mirror, another in the top corner inside the smoke detector, and one more looking down on the room from a light fitting, so the entire room could be seen – and one in the bathroom, poking out of a small hole I had hammered into the wall. There were seven microphones, one in every light fitting and one inside the lamp beside the bed. I could hear the room better than they could. I could see her from the back and the front, depending on which monitor I was looking at. She turned to look at herself in the mirror and adjusted her dress while he went to answer the door. The image of her in front of me was in colour but slightly washed out. If the light caught her skin in the right way, it looked blue.

Due to an internal investigation that had started a month previously, there was also a monitor off to the side that showed the hotel room next door to theirs, room 804, where I was sitting with my colleague L and being recorded. I stared at the back of my head as it looked at a monitor that projected the back of my head, and onwards and onwards, falling down into infinity.

He gave the guy at the door a ten-dollar note and carried the champagne bottle in its silver ice basin over to the bed. I could hear the ice cubes as they clinked against each other. It made my teeth hurt. He had been getting to know her for almost two weeks. They had met at yoga class; he had told her that his name was Michael but it wasn't really. He had taken her out to dinner twice. At first we were going to put a wire on him, just in case she whispered something into his ear and we missed it. He was dressed in a shirt and tie. He had told her that he was an investment banker, something that was suitably of no interest to anybody. He had refused to wear the wire. He'd said even the idea of it made him nervous.

'Make yourself comfortable,' he said now, in the room, and gestured towards the bed.

She sat on the corner of the mattress and looked around. Her eyes were lined and her lips were red. She looked at the lamp. It gave off an orange light.

'This lamp is strange,' she said.

'How do you mean?'

'The décor, it doesn't suit the rest of the room.'

'I hadn't noticed,' he said.

'It doesn't matter.'

He poured champagne into one of the long-stemmed glasses that had come with the bottle. He overfilled it and foam spilled over the edge of the glass and the wet sound of it hitting the carpet made me feel slightly ill.

'Oops,' he said.

She wasn't watching. She was propped up on the bed by her elbows. I found her disinterest in him attractive. I had looked through her chest of drawers and lifted and smelled each item of clothing. She kept the sweaters she would never wear in the drawer that was the second from the bottom. A photo of her and her sister had been tucked into the tight gap between the mirror on top of the chest of drawers and its frame. I had made sure I folded everything back perfectly. I had taken off my gloves only twice, once to touch her pillow, and again to run my finger down the glass door of her shower. Her house was spotless and smelled of her perfume.

He handed her a glass of champagne, the one that hadn't overflowed.

'It's a shame the radio doesn't work,' she said.

'Yes. It's a real shame.'

'Maybe you should call the front desk.'

'I don't want them to think I broke it,' he said.

'You broke it?'

'No, but that's what it'll seem like. Either the person before me broke it or ignored it and I'll ignore it, and then the next person in this room will probably ignore it.'

'And so on and so on into infinity,' she said.

There was a not uncomfortable pause. He leaned against the desk with his hand and drank, perhaps a little too quickly. I watched his Adam's apple move in his throat.

'I never like to think about that,' she said. 'I mean about how many people have been in the hotel room and what they've done. The idea of all the conversations that have happened here, whether or not they've changed anything, makes me feel kind of sick. Then there's everything they've touched. Once, when we were on holiday, my parents took us on this underground cave tour and the tour guide used his torch to point out a stalagmite that had been ruined from everyone touching it over time. Just from the oil from their hands. It's horrible what a body can do, even when it's not trying.'

I was tapping a pen between my fingers. My colleague L was sitting silently beside me, doing a crossword on the back page of a newspaper. He was leaning on the back two legs of his chair and every now and then he'd ask, without looking up, if she'd got her tits out yet. I was starting to worry. I had noticed that the image of myself on the monitor in front of me had started to do things a second before I did them. The image of me moved its hand up to run its fingers through its hair then I followed it, like an echo. The image of me turned around and looked directly at me, almost quizzically, and I turned my head to check out if the camera was still working. I decided not to mention anything about this to L.

'Each room is cleaned though,' he was telling her. 'Thoroughly.' Then he paused, took a breath and said, 'But you shouldn't be worrying about something like that,' in such a tone that they both knew what he was talking about.

She smirked at him and raised an eyebrow and he said, too quickly, 'You know, you look kind of tired,' which neatly tore the moment in half.

She emptied her glass with a throwback of her head and placed it on the bedside table, next to the lamp. One of her rings caught the rim of the glass and there was a slight chime. I was falling for her, which I was trying to keep a handle on, though sometimes she did mundane things that made me giddy. The headphones I was wearing covered my ears, but the room would lapse into such a silence that now and then I could only hear the creaking of L's chair as he rocked slowly back and forth.

In the room he moved a little from side to side and it was easy to see that he didn't know where to go next. Sitting next to her on the bed would be awkward. He leaned across the front of her body and kissed her on the mouth. I turned up the volume to hear better.

My image on the monitor put its head down to write something and then continued to watch the monitor in front of it. I tried to make out the words before writing them down on the legal pad in front of me. The gaps between my image on the monitor doing something and me following its lead were getting longer. This was something I was trying to ignore.

In the room he said, 'You're shaking.'

'It's cold in here.'

'I'm sorry, I forgot about the air conditioning.'

'It's all right,' she said, looking off to the side, straight at the camera. 'I had a dream last night about my bedroom, in fact I was in my bed asleep, dreaming about being in bed. Running along one of my walls is a cupboard with mirrored doors, and I dreamed that there was someone inside with the door just slid open a crack. So they were staring at me, it was a man, and I could see his face and it wasn't an ugly face and it wasn't a beautiful face, it was just plain and calm. I think that made it worse.'

'Probably,' he said gently, sounding confused.

She smiled and picked up her purse. 'Forget it,' she said. 'I'll be right back,' and she stood up and kissed him quickly again and walked towards the bathroom. Her hips swayed as she walked.

'I'll just make myself comfortable,' he said and when her back was turned he looked at the mirror and gave the camera – or me, really – a wink.

She kept a shoebox under her bed. The first thing I noticed about it was that unlike everything else under there – magazines in piles, a few pairs of shoes, a flat plastic box filled with ski wear – the shoebox was completely free of dust. Inside it were photographs of her and various men in pornographic positions. Most of the photos were of men tied to her bed frame with different coloured silk scarves, the same scarf never appeared twice, and neither did any of the men. There were a few photos of her naked, but with a scarf wrapped tightly around her head, showing the hollow dents of her eyes and the soft pyramid of her nose.

She stood and looked at herself in the bathroom mirror. She pulled lightly at her face with a forefinger and thumb and stretched her cheeks out. It looked like her face was made of clay. In the bedroom he was reclined on the bed, his shoes still on the floor, his arms bent at triangles so that his fingers could twine themselves together at the back of his head. He seemed relaxed; his toes were twitching in time to, I guessed, the same tune his fingers had tapped out before. She was breathing deeply in the bathroom, but she looked calm. When I turned up the volume on the bathroom microphone I could hear that she was talking to herself. I turned the dial up even more until there were pops and cracks and I caught her voice repeating; 'It's okay, it's okay, it's okay.' There was a flash of something thin and metallic in her purse which her fingers rearranged. The purse snapped shut. I had forgotten to turn the volume down and as she left the closing of the bathroom door resonated in my headphones like a gunshot. On the monitor of the room I was sitting in, the image of me was scrambling to pull its headphones off and L had gotten up so fast to run to the door that he accidentally knocked over his chair.

Giraffe

My girlfriend's uncle shows me a photo album filled mostly with naked pictures of his ex-wives. He's been divorced four times now so there's a lot of photographs. Rachel has stepped outside to take a phone call; as soon as she walked out the door her uncle called me over and pulled the album down from the top shelf of his only bookcase. I want Rachel to come back. Her uncle flips the pages without saying anything. I am half-sure that she is outside talking to her lover; I'm still not sure he exists, but I've been obsessing over him for weeks.

'Well Chris,' he says. 'What do you think of that?'

I'm quiet for a second. It's an interesting question because I don't actually know what to think. The photographs are tastefully done, lots of the women are posed quite well and artfully looking off into the distance. There are a few landscapes thrown in there for good measure, as a break from the naked women, and also three photographs of a giraffe in an enclosure at a zoo. I tell him that he seems to have a pretty good command of light.

For the last two summers Rachel and I have been driving to her uncle's farm to help him cut down and sell Christmas trees. This year, though, a disease has gotten to them and they've turned brown and dry. Rachel wanted to drive out here anyway. When we arrive the first thing we do is go look at them, standing in the low corner of a big empty field. The branches are bare and look like burned-up matchsticks and make no sound at all in the breeze. They don't smell like pine either.

Rachel's uncle has set up a beach chair so he can sit and watch them. He says it's been hard for a while, but now he's started to come to terms with it.

It took us two days to drive out here. In the car, with the windows down and our backs sweating, Rachel played her learn-to-speak German cassette tapes endlessly. I did try to follow along, but soon enough I'd lose interest and look out the window and worry. I was convinced she was playing these tapes so she could talk without having a conversation. I wondered if she was seeing a man from Germany. I hit pause on the tape player.

'I suppose your uncle is pretty sad about these trees,' I said.

'I've been thinking about getting him a dog,' Rachel

said and then turned the tape player back on by jabbing it with her thumb.

She's the only person in her family who still talks to her uncle. I know that her parents are pretty much done with him. He once owned a chain of electronics stores, but they went bankrupt almost a decade ago and since then he's never held another steady job. He was a builder for a time, and then he tried to make and sell pottery. Rachel still has the vase he made us sitting on our kitchen counter, even though the thing doesn't hold water for longer than a day.

There have also been the Christmas trees every December, though that hasn't really panned out this time around.

Rachel comes back inside and her uncle closes the photo album and puts it back. I don't say anything, just look at her, and she says, 'It was work,' and holds up her phone. I don't know why her uncle showed me his photographs but he's red-faced from drinking beer most of the afternoon and, when he notices that Rachel isn't watching, he winks at me in a way that I wish he wouldn't.

Rachel and her uncle don't look anything alike.

Outside there's the buzzing of insects that sound like heat. The house is half-finished; there's a blue tarp covering one end of the lounge room and there are Christmas lights running over the door frame and strung up across the ceiling so it looks like a net. Now and then a breeze will push against the tarp and flutter it. Even though it's daytime the lights are on and blinking rapidly.

'Now that you're here there isn't much to do, not with the trees in such a state,' he says.

'It's nice to be here anyway,' Rachel says.

There's an arrangement of white tinsel attached to the house's front door by a staple gun. The land around here is so flat it makes me uneasy. We should have bought him a dog. Rachel's uncle has two grey horses, which were so sick when he got them that he couldn't bring himself to name them, and they still look too skinny out there in the heat, with their heads down, dreaming, or looking at you with their big wet expectant eyes. It always surprises me, when I'm close up, that you don't hear the sound of a broken accordion when they breathe in and out.

Sometimes I wonder how he can stand to be living in a place like this. What a holiday! I'll walk in on Rachel and her uncle talking together quietly and they'll hush up all of a sudden and look at me with expressions so similar that it's easy to see they're related. Sometimes they'll be laughing and I'll ask them what's so funny, but Rachel will shake her head and tell me that it's too hard to explain, I just had to be there.

On the last day I'll take an axe to a few of those dead trees and whack them down, and they'll fall easy but it won't feel as good as I think it will. On the trip home we'll stay at a cheap, pink-walled motel. The room will have a waterbed and Rachel will lie on it, frowning up at the ceiling and bouncing herself up and down. I will be standing at the window, using the motel phone, trying to call my mother to tell her I'll be flying down for the holidays. My mother will be either knitting in front of the television or asleep in front of the television. I will be pushing the curtains apart gently, watching a man in the motel's car park drag a folded stroller into the back of his car. I'll be listening to the phone ring out, waiting for my mother to pick up.

Travelling through the air

Beckman's uncle George picked them up on the street to drive them to the airport. He'd called before arriving and told Beckman and his mother to be out the front in five minutes. He'd said, 'It's just like a real taxi service, hey?' and then hung up before Beckman could reply. It was a Monday morning. They'd been staying at his cousin's over the weekend and were flying back home around ten. Their tickets had been cheaper this way.

George drove his wife's station wagon in an agitated kind of way. He changed lanes often. Beckman had never been in a car with him before, so he didn't know if this was the way he always drove.

'I'm happy to take the morning off, it helps that I'm virtually self-employed now,' George said. 'If I want to go play golf, then I'm right out there on the fairway. If an emergency comes up or I feel like going to the movies, no problem. I don't have a soul to answer to.'

'It sounds pretty good,' Beckman said.

'Is work going well? Are you back there this week?'

He nodded and said, 'Yes. It's great,' and then nothing more. Although George was talkative, Beckman always found him a struggle to talk to. It didn't help that Beckman was out of a job and so far he'd said nothing to anyone about it. He'd teach his fiction classes for two more weeks, but there wouldn't be a position for him in the coming semester. He'd planned on telling his mother this while they were travelling together, but whenever he'd thought about it he'd ended up wanting to curl up and fall asleep.

In the back seat his mother was quiet and looking out the window. She was wearing lipstick and earrings and still liked to dress well for air travel.

They'd flown down for his mother's aunt's birthday. She had turned ninety. There'd been a party at her place and now, weaving through traffic, Beckman could easily recall the look of displeasure on her face when the birthday cake had been put down in front of her.

In the airport's car park George climbed out and lifted their suitcase from the boot. Beckman's mother grabbed it off him before he could put it down and said, 'Thank you, I've got it from here.'

George nodded to the both of them. 'I forget how strong you are sometimes. You should have seen her when she was younger,' George said to Beckman. 'She used to be able to whack a nail into a wall with one hit.'

'That's not true,' his mother said.

'The other kids used to come around to see her amazing feats of strength.'

Beckman's mother didn't say anything, but walked ahead of them in silence, and George looked over at Beckman and nodded his head with his eyebrows raised and his eyes closed. They walked across the car park and as soon as they entered the terminal George said he needed to use the bathroom.

'No one ever thinks I can do anything,' his mother said once George was out of earshot. 'They act so nice because they think I'm old, but that's worse. It's much worse. You just wait.'

'He was only being friendly,' Beckman said.

'I don't need friendly anymore. I have enough friends.'

After checking in their suitcases and going through security, they had half an hour to pass. The three of them went to the bar near their departure gate. They sat at a table in the corner. The walls around them were glass and Beckman watched three planes take off, one after another. He liked to think he was a rational person, but each time an aeroplane left the ground it seemed like it was lifted into the air by magic rather than engineering. He'd bought himself a whisky and slugged it down at the bar, then taken a beer back to their table. He drank it as fast as possible; he was hoping to get at least one more in by the time they'd boarded the plane.

'Beckman, you'll make yourself sick,' his mother said.

'I'll take sick over anxious,' he said. 'Or fear.'

'If the idea of getting your stomach pumped when you're a kilometre up in the air doesn't scare you,' George said, 'then I don't know what will.'

'I don't like flying,' Beckman said.

'No, I know,' his mother said. 'When he was a kid we used to have this kite, do you remember?'

'Not really.'

'He used to have a fit if anyone ever flew it. He'd work himself into hysterics. He and his father used to fight about it every time it was windy and his father wanted to fly it in the park. Beckman would beg him to leave it on his bedroom wall. You really don't remember that?'

'No,' he said. 'I guess there's a lot of things I've forgotten.'

'It comes with age,' George said.

Beckman looked over to their gate, where about twenty people were standing in a row, most of them alone, staring into space. A few people were wearing suits and had newspapers folded under their arms. Since his father died his mother had moved house seven times. She was retired and on a pension, so none of the moves had been brought on by economic necessity, it was just that every eight months or so she'd pack everything up and go to a different house.

Whenever she called on him to help her move her belongings, Beckman always agreed to without asking why she was going through it all over again.

'Maybe we should line up,' Beckman said.

'Soon, but not yet. Relax a little,' his mother said. 'I don't see why everyone's in such a hurry. No matter how fast you find your seat the plane's not going to take off any faster or slower. Do people know that?'

Beckman finished his drink and started peeling off the bottle's label. His mother was making a point, he thought, of taking her time. Their flight was announced and Beckman took his glasses off and put them on the table. He was thankful that his mother hadn't yet mentioned that they used to belong to his father.

'Showtime,' George said. 'I'll hang around here until you guys take off.'

'You should wave at us,' Beckman's mother said.

'I'll shout at you like I'm on the dock and you're on a cruise.'

Beckman felt ill. He wanted to order another beer, but they didn't have enough time. The sky outside was clear and held aeroplanes.

'I need you to come by once your classes are over,' his mother said to him. 'My shower is clogged and I want you to take a look at it. At the moment I'm showering under a trickle.'

'I can pay for a plumber,' Beckman said, because he was starting to feel guilty every time she mentioned his work.

'Who says you can't fix it? I'm sure you would have made a fine plumber.'

'What about Robert?'

'He was supposed to be an electrician.'

Beckman felt angry at his brother then, for no real reason other than that he wasn't around; Robert didn't like dealing with anything at all family related and he always made the excuse he was busy at work.

'You'd get pretty good money,' George said. 'For doing something like that. Still, though, you could probably afford it on a university salary.'

Beckman nodded and looked away from his uncle's gleaming, too-earnest face. He wondered what would happen if, right then, George happened to explode.

Once they'd said goodbye to George – after he'd clapped Beckman on the shoulder roughly and called him 'Captain' – and once they'd lined up and then walked across the tarmac and up the thin, ladder-like staircase into the rear of the plane, Beckman hunched in the aisle to look for their seat numbers. A man wearing a pocket-covered khaki vest was already sitting in the window seat of their row. He looked like he was on safari. Beckman nodded at him once, then ushered his mother into the middle seat. He sat down in the aisle seat, clicked on his seatbelt and put a stick of gum in his mouth.

'It was nice of George to drive us,' his mother said, after she'd sat down and arranged herself.

'Yeah, it was,' Beckman said. 'He's good value.'

'I know he's financially secure but I still think he's miserable.'

When the plane taxied down the runway the flight attendants went through the safety instructions. They told everyone to watch, even if they'd flown before, and Beckman stared at them, trying to look attentive, though he was thinking about the time he walked across the campus one night and there had been spotlights beautifully illuminating the university's sandstone walls. It had been cold and a choir had been standing around outside, practising in their scarves, and Beckman had been overwhelmed by the kind of sentimentality he'd been spending most of the semester trying to eradicate from his students' work. He felt guilty that this was something he couldn't share with his mother. It was the kind of anecdote she usually enjoyed.

'I hate this bit,' his mother said when the plane paused before it picked up speed for take-off. 'Everything else I'm fine with. Just this bit.'

Beckman nodded. He arranged and then rearranged

his feet on the floor in front of him, trying to make them somehow feel right. There was a rush as they accelerated down the runway; the front of the plane tilted upwards and then they were in the air. Beckman looked out the window at the roofs of houses, and as they climbed higher he saw the deep blue of the harbour and, further out, the ocean. The plane shuddered and started to level out.

'Well, I'm glad that's over,' his mother said.

'Not yet,' Beckman said.

The fasten seatbelt light was still on above their heads. His mother put her hand on his forearm. He realised he was gripping onto his armrests. He loosened his grip and let go and then rubbed his hands.

'They're cramped now,' he said.

'You shouldn't be wearing your father's glasses either, you'll ruin your eyes.'

'I can see pretty well with them.'

Her own glasses made her eyes look bigger and sadder than they really were. She said, 'Your hands wouldn't hurt if you ate more bananas.'

He heard the clean metallic click of a seatbelt being released behind him and someone bumped into the back of his seat as they tried to get up. A flight attendant said, 'Please stay seated.'

'Okay,' a woman's voice said.

'Just until the seatbelt light has been switched off.'

Beckman looked through the gap between his seat

and his mother's but he couldn't see much, just movement now and then. Even so, he could tell the woman behind him was agitated. Now and then he could hear her voice, but not what she was saying.

They rose above the clouds. Out of the window now it looked like a snow-covered field, with gaps like pools of water that fell back down to the ground.

The seatbelt light went off. The woman behind him immediately got up, again bumping his seat, and headed for the bathroom at the rear of the plane. Beckman leaned into the aisle to see her, but he didn't get a good look at her, just her dress and long dark hair. He straightened himself back into his seat.

'What's happening?' his mother said.

'Nothing,' Beckman said. 'I don't know, I can't see anything.'

'Maybe she's going to throw up.'

'Maybe,' he said.

His ears were blocked and he kept chewing his gum, but he didn't mind the feeling so much. It made him feel like he was floating, his head half-submerged, in the bath. He coughed to clear his head. His mother looked like she was about to fall asleep.

Later, inside the aeroplane's cabin, he was lulled by the hum of the engines. It was a comfort. Down the aisle, towards the front of the cabin, the flight attendants had brought out the food cart. Beckman checked his wallet, but he hadn't thought to keep any money on him. He spat out his gum into a tissue and put two more pieces in his mouth. In an hour or so they'd be back on the ground.

The flight attendants progressed through the rows. The cart came to their row and each of them – Beckman, his mother, the man in the safari suit – politely shook their heads.

The woman who'd been seated behind him was still in the bathroom. Beckman wondered if he should tell anyone about her. He worried he was the only one who had noticed her absence. Maybe she was travelling alone.

'I think I feel like a wine,' his mother said.

'Do you want me to call for one?' Beckman said. 'They're not that far down the aisle, I could call out.'

'No, don't. I'll be home soon. I drank enough at the airport.'

Beckman thought of his mother's house, and how she had moved her television into the bedroom so she wouldn't have to get up most of the day. Whenever he visited he always ended up sitting on her double bed late at night, on the side she never occupied, watching it, with her asleep beside him. She said that she fell asleep every night with the television going.

The food cart finished its run. The woman still hadn't returned. Beckman heard the overhead compartment above him open. A flight attendant was rummaging through it and Beckman turned to look at her. When she reached her shirt rode up a little and he saw a flash of tanned skin, just above her hip. He looked away.

'Excuse me, did anyone see that woman's bag?' the flight attendant said. 'She said it was small and purple.'

'Under the seat,' a man's voice said.

The overhead compartment was closed. Beckman's mother leaned over him and said to the flight attendant, 'What's going on?'

'Nothing serious. The woman who was sitting here just needs some medication.'

'Can I help?'

'She had a diabetic fit.'

'I'm a nurse, I have training,' Beckman's mother said. 'If you need a hand let me know.'

'Thank you. We'll let you know if you can help,' the flight attendant said, and walked back to the rear of the plane, carrying the woman's small purple bag.

'What's happening?'

'I don't think they want my help.'

Beckman's mother had never been a nurse, he wasn't sure if she'd even done first aid training. He didn't say anything and his mother pulled the in-flight magazine from the pocket on the seat in front of her. She flicked through it.

'You see?' she said, sounding unimpressed. 'Someone's already filled out the crossword in here. You'd think they could replace the magazines once they're done.'

The plane started to descend. He thought that now was probably the right time to come clean with his mother. Outside of the window was suddenly grey. This was usually when Beckman felt worry overcome him, when he was convinced that the world below had suddenly vanished. He'd think about the people in the aeroplane being the only things left, circling around where the planet had been. His mother coughed beside him and kept turning the pages of her magazine and Beckman waited for the plane to dip back down from out of the clouds.

Athletics

I'd spent most of the week sitting around my house, waiting for my ex-girlfriend Catherine to call. I'd lied to my work and told them I was sick from food poisoning. Mostly during this time I was feeling sorry for myself, watching television or eating or checking my email. Sometimes I would go for walks, or stand in my kitchen and watch boats on the river down the hill, but it had been raining most of the time and I was really only afforded a view of wet trees and the occasional soaked bird sitting plump and grey on the railing of my veranda. I felt like I was wasting time.

On Thursday, around noon, my brother Adam called me. We hadn't spoken in a while, though we kept a loose line of contact with each other. He usually sent a postcard or made a few phone calls around Christmas. He never sent me anything for my birthday. I was surprised to hear from him.

I said 'Adam, hello' and then he launched into a speech as though he was being interviewed. He told me that he was calling from a phone booth because the commune he was living at didn't have a phone. He said that he was watching the raindrops wriggle down the outside of the booth like tadpoles.

I listened to him and looked at the phone cord that attached the receiver to the phone, then followed the line that came out of the phone to where it connected to the wall. It made me think of the plant that had sprung up in the floor of my shower, between the tiles. At first the idea that there were plants holding my place together had been a pleasant one, and then I'd torn the weed out and felt its damp grittiness, like river silt, and the whole thing had made me feel nauseous.

I waited long enough to seem polite and then said, 'So what's the problem?'

'Nothing,' Adam said. 'Nothing terrible, but I was wondering if maybe you'd do me a huge favour and drive down here to pick me up.'

'Right now?' I said.

'That would probably be for the best, yeah.'

I looked outside at the rain. It wasn't heavy but it was constant, and I could hear the comforting tap-tap-tap of water on my rooftop. The sun was out there somewhere, though I couldn't see it exactly. I said, 'I'm not going to turn up there and all of a sudden you've changed your mind, right?'

'Trust me,' Adam said. 'There's no chance of that happening at all.'

He gave me directions and I copied them down on the back of an envelope. He was somewhere south, just over the border, in one of the valleys scattered throughout the hinterland. His voice grew quieter the more we talked, which meant he was upset. I wasn't going to mention it, but I hoped that he'd ask me what I was doing home in the middle of the week, and then I could tell him about staying indoors and Catherine leaving me. I hadn't left the house for days.

Adam didn't ask, and before hanging up I told him I'd be there as soon as possible. I went and put on a different t-shirt and an old jacket and a pair of sneakers. I left on my tracksuit pants because I didn't think they looked so bad. They were black and had two white stripes running down each leg. I looked both formal and athletic, like maybe I owned a gym.

The drive down was unremarkable and I listened to the radio and watched the wipers lean towards each other, never touching, back and forth across the windscreen. Catherine had broken up with me in a café down near the beach. She had a cold and pulled a tissue from her sleeve. She'd had her light brown hair cut short the week before and it suited her very well. She ordered lemon tea.

'I might get some eggs,' I said.

'If you want to order food you can, but I don't feel like eating.'

'Do you want half of what I order?'

'No, I'm not hungry.'

'Are you sure? Will you want to eat my food once you smell it?'

Catherine was silent for a moment before she said, 'I'm leaving you.' Then she put a nasal inhaler in her right nostril, sprayed it, then did the same with the left.

The sea was green-blue and choppy. People on surfboards were floating out behind the small waves. We hadn't been together for very long. Catherine cupped her hand over her mouth and coughed.

Now, in the car, the road was mostly empty and I took the corners carefully. I didn't like to drive fast in the rain. When I finally made it to the commune the rain had eased off a bit, but everything was still wet. I drove up a long driveway, through the middle of a field that was empty apart from a few unconnected fence posts and a tractor missing both of its back wheels and pointing skywards. At the end of the driveway there was an old two-storey farmhouse made from dull-grey wood. There were lights on inside, and in one of the upstairs windows. The window frames looked rusted out, and some of the beams over the front veranda were curling from rot, but other than that the place didn't look too bad. I'd imagined worse.

Adam was sitting out the front, slumped in a deckchair, with his arms across his chest. When he saw me he stood and held his hand up in the air, then turned and called out something through the open doorway before walking over to my car with his rucksack. He tossed the bag onto the back seat and then sat down in the passenger seat. A fat man came and stood in the farmhouse doorway, his head slightly tilted upwards and his arms resting on each side of the door frame, watching as I turned the car around in the driveway and headed towards the road.

'I can't thank you enough,' Adam said.

'It's no problem,' I said. 'The rain slowed me down a bit.'

'I'm freezing, does this car have heating?'

I nodded and Adam leaned forwards and messed with the dials until he had the heat going. He sat back in his seat. It started to rain again. He smelled damp and the mohair jumper he was wearing had small, silver beads of moisture hanging from its fibres.

'Maybe you should take your jumper off,' I said.

'It was a nice place, there was a stream out the back. It was peaceful,' he said. 'But I really had to get out of there.'

'Why, what happened?' I said.

Adam took his seatbelt off and pulled his jumper over his head. 'Nothing serious,' he said. 'They had a generator, but the only things it powered were the light bulbs. Plus everything either in or around the place was always damp.'

'Did they have running water?'

'I mentioned the stream, didn't I?'

Adam leaned forward and turned the volume up on the stereo, which spiked loud enough to make the speakers rattle, then he turned it back down low. The windows were starting to fog from the heat, so I adjusted the car's air conditioning until cold air blew from the vents and the white clouds on the windshield started to clear.

'But I was having a hard time there,' he said. 'I kept thinking that the other people on the commune were going to come into my room during the night and strangle me with my belt.'

'And they never did anything?' I said.

'Yeah, it was mostly in my head. I was convinced they would either choke me or poison my food. I know it sounds stupid, but they didn't have TV or a radio or anything. At night it was so dark, I mean, that kind of thing can really get to you.'

'You're okay though?'

'Me? Yeah, I'm fine. I'm starving though. We should stop somewhere and eat.'

I explained to Adam that I didn't feel like stopping. We were over two hours away from my place, probably even longer because of the rain. It was starting to get late. The road was empty and wound around hills and dipped into valleys. There wasn't much around except the occasional farmhouse, driveway or burned-out hollow tree stump. Adam and I drove mostly in a silence, with the wipers going and the radio turned down low.

The first sign of trouble was the red and blue flashing lights catching in the rain on the windshield. I slowed the car down to a roll and Adam said, 'Oh boy,' in a defeated kind of way. Ahead of us, parked across the road, was a Land Cruiser with police lights blinking silently on its roof. A policeman wearing a raincoat and a hat with a wide brim was standing next to the Land Cruiser and hailing us. I stopped the car.

While I wound down my window and the policeman walked over to our car, I had the thought that he was here to take Adam away and I felt a short pang of guilt over how relieved that made me feel. The policeman put his arm up on my roof casually and leaned down to look at us through my open window. Rain ran down the inside of my door.

'Sorry, guys, but you're going to have to head back. The river down there's overflowing,' he said, gesturing down the road to somewhere out of sight. 'Most of the bridge is under water. Luckily I haven't seen too many people around.'

'Was there any significant property damage?' Adam said, leaning towards the window.

The policeman either didn't hear or ignored him and said, 'We're cutting the road off up here as a precaution.'

'Well,' I said, trying to appear cheery, 'if there's nothing that can be done.'

The policeman patted the roof of my car three times, like you would a horse, and headed back to his Land Cruiser. I wound my window up, then reversed and swung the car around.

We drove back past the turn-off to Adam's commune, and into a small town close by. I stopped at a service station that had a takeaway restaurant. When I killed the engine I sat for a moment, listening to the rain hit the car roof.

'Now you can get something to eat,' I said.

'There's supposed to be a better place on the other side of town,' Adam said. 'They might be closed, though, so I guess this place will do.'

I got out of the car and Adam followed. We walked quickly, hunched over in the rain, and in through the service station's automatic glass doors. The inside of the restaurant was carpeted and smelled like the vomitous air that came out the back of a vacuum cleaner. At the counter Adam ordered a hamburger and I bought a Coke. We took a seat at one of the white plastic tables. It wasn't very clean; there were spots of black dirt fossilised to the tabletop.

When we were younger, when I was sixteen and Adam was fourteen, we had gone through a weird kind of follow the leader. I had been the one to teach him about drinking, about smoking and drug use and sex. But where he'd smoked steady jets of smoke behind the bus stop at school, I had coughed and spluttered; and where he'd said the whisky we'd sneaked at my uncle's barbecue had burned a little, he'd still seemed unfazed, while I'd felt something awful rise in my throat and had thrown up into the bathtub.

By the time Adam's hamburger was ready I'd finished my drink and was staring out the window. I was rotating my empty can on the tabletop, the can turned slightly on its side like a loose tyre about to spin to the ground.

'They didn't let me have meat out there,' Adam said, lifting his hamburger.

'Really?'

'Well, not exactly, but none of them ate meat and there was this real kind of judgement thing going on. You couldn't cook meat in any of their pans, or use their plates or cutlery, because then it would taint them with suffering.'

'Suffering?'

'Yeah, one of the guys there, Richard, actually said that to me. So now and then I'd sneak into town and eat a steak. One time I spiked their lentil soup with blood. Not a lot of blood. I know it sounds wrong, and it was probably a bad thing to do, but it kept me sane.'

Apart from the rain, the bottom of the Coke can slowly spinning on the tabletop was the only sound to be heard.

'It's hardly my fault,' Adam said.

'I know,' I said. 'It's not that.'

'Then what? I said you didn't have to come get me if you didn't want to.'

'Don't worry about it,' I said. 'You know I wasn't going to leave you stranded out here.'

When Adam had graduated from high school I'd still been living with our parents. Adam had gone off and tried out a number of things — working on a tuna boat, selling fruit on the side of the highway, making pillows in a factory — but none of these things had ever seemed to stick. He was definitely always the black sheep. Where I had planned, he had always schemed. His last proper job had been at a car rental booth at an airport.

Sometimes I wondered why my life was so stable and his was a mess. Other times I worried that he was a genius and I was wasting my life.

Adam finished his hamburger and crumpled his wrapper into a ball. He bounced it weakly into the middle of the table.

'You know, I didn't really like you much when we were growing up,' I said.

'I don't think we were ever supposed to be friends,' he said.

'We were both pretty popular in high school. We were both in the track team.'

'I don't think that made a difference.'

I nodded and stood up and told Adam I had to make a phone call. My mobile phone didn't have any reception, but there was a public phone over near the counter. I dropped in some change and dialled Catherine's number. The phone started ringing on the other end and after about three rings I lost my nerve and ended the call. I could see Adam over at the table, throwing the wrapper a short distance into the air and then catching it. He did it over and over without distraction. I pretended to have a conversation. I said, 'Hello?' to the dial tone and then kept saying 'Okay' over and over again, nodding with my head down, as though I was being lectured. After about a minute of this I hung up, collected my change from the phone, and then went into the small bathroom and looked at myself in the mirror. I felt suddenly exhausted. The bar of soap sitting beside the sink was mostly mush and I squeezed my hand into it, like soft clay, down to its firm centre.

When I returned to our table the wrapper was gone and so was my empty can. Adam was leaning with his arms crossed and both his elbows up on the table. I stood behind my chair.

'Look,' Adam said. 'There's that policeman.'

I looked out the service station window to the petrol pumps, where the Land Cruiser was now parked. The automatic doors opened and the policeman walked inside, shaking rainwater from his hat.

He ordered a coffee and started chatting with the woman behind the counter. When he noticed Adam and me he gave us both a nod and kept on with his conversation.

When his coffee came, in a white polystyrene cup, he fixed a lid onto it and walked back out to his car. The policeman drove off and headed in the opposite direction, away from the roadblock. I told Adam that we were leaving. After we'd run through the rain and hopped into the car, I pulled out of the car park and headed down the road, back out of town.

'What are you doing?' Adam said. 'The bridge is out, remember?'

'I know,' I said.

'Then where are we going?'

I didn't answer. I drove back along the road, a little faster this time. I had the windscreen wipers going full bore. I slowed down when I saw a white wooden barricade sitting across the middle of the road. There wasn't a sign of anyone else around. I figured there wasn't much of a police force in a place like this. Down the hill I could see, in a dense, ink-black area, the river.

'You see, let's just go back, okay?' Adam said.

'Come and help me, we'll move it,' I said.

'Why?'

'Actually, you stay here and drive through once I clear the way. The faster we do this the better.'

Adam didn't say anything and I jumped out of the

car. I ran through the rain and over to the barricade. It was cold outside and the air smelled rich. I lifted the thick wooden beam, which was heavy but not as heavy as I'd expected, and shuffled it over to clear the road. Rain was hitting me everywhere. I leaned up and waved Adam through. Once the car had passed me I returned the barricade back into position. When I climbed into the car Adam had already shifted back over to the passenger seat.

'Simple,' I said.

The surface of the bridge had vanished, but the guard rails were still sticking up out of the water like the remains of a jetty. I accelerated down towards it.

When we hit the bridge, water fanned out from the car, thrown up by the tyres. There was a smooth, clear sound underneath our feet. Adam inhaled quickly and put his hand on the dashboard to steady himself. I felt for a second that the car might float away and we'd be carried off, but then I felt the tyres catch on the road and we emerged from the water.

'Man, that was close,' Adam said, and then laughed.

I continued on up the road, leaving the river behind us. I felt a single sharp heartbeat of disappointment at our safety. I started to picture what we'd do back at my place. I didn't have much food in the house, and I worried about what Adam would think, looking at the shelves of my barren refrigerator.

'Can you pull over for a second?' Adam said.

'Where?'

'Just here.'

I pulled over, beside a ditch. Adam opened his door and hopped out. He walked to the middle of the road, bent over with both his hands on his knees, and threw up. He straightened, then bent over and threw up again. I got out of the car and walked towards him. The rain was coming down pretty heavily and it was making his sick run towards the edge of the road, over to the car. I stepped around it and put my hand on Adam's shoulder. He was still hunched over and spitting onto the ground.

'Are you okay?' I said.

'I don't think that hamburger agreed with me,' he said.

'I'm sorry.'

Adam reached up and tapped my hand. It felt like when we were younger and he was bent over on the starting block before a race, waiting for the pistol to fire, before he ran and ran and ran.

Sleeping with the light on

The first boy Lillian ever slept with lived two houses down from her and played tennis after school. Sometimes she'd see him walking home from the bus stop dressed in his whites. They didn't really know each other that well, but their mothers were friends. They'd slept together when Lillian had come home between semesters, in her second year of university. His name was Tim Miller and for a while Lillian's mother would mention what he was doing in her letters. Tim was flying jets for the air force. Tim was married now, also like Lillian. Her mother wrote to her often and Lillian rarely sent anything back.

She was thinking about Tim and, more specifically, the shape of his hands, while she stood in the kitchen. Her husband James was in the kitchen too, emptying the last few drops of wine into his glass by turning the bottle upside down and shaking it dry. Lillian had been feeling exhausted all week. No matter how much sleep she managed to get, the inside of her head still felt as dull as cotton. James said something that she didn't catch.

'What?' she said.

'I was saying that you don't look so good.'

'I'm fine,' she said.

The pot was boiling on the stove. The lid rattled and there was water bubbling at its rim, spitting onto the stovetop. James slowly folded a tea towel over in his hand and lifted the lid, looking inside.

'Do you want me to do something with this?' he said.

The first time Lillian had gone to James's place he'd made pasta, but since then he had really only ever cooked one meal a year for her, the same meal, on her birthday. It was something he took very seriously, even though it wasn't that difficult to fry zucchini and make a light cream sauce. It involved only one egg.

'No, it's fine,' she said, taking the chopping board of cleaned potatoes and pushing them into the water with a knife. She shook in some salt.

James said, 'What are we supposed to talk about anyway?'

'They're nice people,' Lillian said. 'I'm sure it'll be easy.'

About a week ago their neighbours, Hannah and Franklin, had been broken into. When Lillian had heard about it from Hannah she'd invited them both over for dinner. They'd lived next door to each other for years, but still, Lillian and James didn't know them very well.

She started to cut up an onion. Then she cut up a capsicum.

'I don't see why, just because someone broke into their house, you had to invite them over.'

'I don't know either,' Lillian said. 'It just seemed like the right thing to do.'

She continued cutting. The onions made her eyes sting. She could tell James was thinking it over, he looked like he was chewing. It always made her anxious when he was this deep in thought. He had trouble letting things go.

'They're at least five years older than us,' he said finally.

'So?' she said. 'What's that got to do with anything?'

'I'm not saying it's a problem, I'm just saying that we're younger.'

Lillian shrugged. James got on well with people and found it easy to talk to strangers, but over the course of ten or so years of marriage he'd slowly managed to cut most of his friends out of his life. Sometimes Lillian worried this was her fault.

'We should get really drunk before they get here,' he said. 'Like really hammered.'

'Hammered?' she said.

'Yeah, so at least then we'll be interesting.'

'We are interesting,' Lillian said, 'and that wouldn't

work anyway, when you get drunk you become so incredibly quiet.'

She drained the potatoes in the sink, then started frying the onion and capsicum in a pan on the stove. She added garlic, vinegar and chilli. James was leaning up against the kitchen bench and slowing turning his wineglass in his hand.

She was sleeping with Tim Miller again. They'd run into each other by accident at a hardware store two months ago. He was bigger than she remembered. Not so much fatter, just wider and taller, though he still had no trouble hitting a tennis ball, as he'd shown her one evening on the roof of his apartment building. He'd bounced the ball twice on the ground, thrown it a short distance into the air, then smacked it up onto the roof of the neighbouring building.

He wasn't flying planes anymore. Instead he owned a sporting goods store. The apartment was his, he'd bought it as an investment and as a place to stay if he ever worked late in the city. It wasn't a very big place, and it always smelled of baking. She'd asked him about it once, in bed.

'It's a trick I learned,' he'd said. 'Half an hour before someone arrives you stick a croissant in the oven and heat it up.'

'Really?' Lillian had said.

'Or a muffin. I picked it up from our real estate agent when my wife and I were trying to sell our house. She flipped over the idea and started doing it all the time. Whenever we'd have guests over she'd shove something in the oven.'

Lillian had lifted up Timothy's arm and bit him then, hoping that he'd think she was being playful, though really she'd done it because she wanted him to keep quiet about things like that.

'Are you done with that?' James said, nodding towards the dishes that were stacked neatly beside the sink.

'Yes,' Lillian said.

He moved to the sink, poured in a bit of detergent and turned on the taps. White foam, like a child's model of Antarctica, bloomed in the water. He pulled on the pair of washing-up gloves that were folded over the neck of the tap. They were bright pink. Lillian started slicing the potatoes.

'What does he do again?' James said.

She'd paused, not entirely sure for a second who he was actually talking about. 'A consultant, I think,' she said. 'Something to do with computers.'

'I should stop thinking about what we're going to talk about. If I do that I'll obsess over it and then my mind will go blank.'

'You shouldn't worry about it,' she said, adding the potatoes to the pan and stirring them quickly.

'It's lucky Hannah doesn't work,' James said. 'I can remember that one easy.'

With the potatoes fried Lillian emptied the pan into a casserole dish and then slid it into the oven, next to the lamb. She stood up straight. James was still washing up; he had his back to her and she could smell the artificial pine of the dishwashing liquid. It made her feel slightly sick.

'Maybe we could tell them that we've heard them having sex,' she said.

'That should be our opener,' he said, pulling the gloves off and hanging them back over the tap. He turned to face her. 'Are you okay? You don't look so good.'

She lifted her wineglass and drank from it. She pictured herself biting down on the glass until it broke, and then the glass in her mouth, which she hated the thought of, but when she was distressed it was usually the kind of thing that came to mind.

She said, 'I think I'm getting a cold.'

'You should take some zinc,' James said. 'I think we have tablets somewhere.'

They kept all their medicine on a shelf near the stove. James looked through the boxes of pills, accidentally knocking a box of Panadol onto the floor.

'It's not looking good,' he said. 'I can go out if you want.'

'No, don't worry about it,' she said.

She put her glass down on the counter and went to the bathroom. She closed the door and locked it.

She took her glasses off, turned the tap on and washed her face, then sat on the toilet with the lid down and waited for three whole minutes.

For almost two months now she had been unemployed, after the arts organisation she worked for had lost a large part of its funding. On her last day her workmates had presented her with a cake with a sad-looking whale on it, drawn in blue icing. It was either crying or asleep, she couldn't tell and didn't ask. Now she was spending most of her time inside the house and making sure never to walk to check the letterbox at the same time as any of their neighbours.

If James ever asked her why she was acting differently she'd blame it on her being fired, but he never asked. She washed her face again, patted it dry with a towel, replaced her glasses and left the bathroom.

James was still in the kitchen. He usually stood around and talked to her while she cooked. This is where we spend the bulk of our time together, Lillian thought. James was standing completely motionless. He sometimes reminded her of a dog her grandfather had owned, which would follow him into town and wait patiently at the door of the supermarket while he shopped.

Because, right then, she hated this small part of him, Lillian walked over and kissed him on the cheek and squeezed his arm a little harder than she meant to.

'Is everything ready?' he said.

'I was going to put cheese out, but I forgot.'

'It's okay,' James said, moving to the cupboard. 'We'll have chips or something.'

'I was going to let it soften,' she said.

Lillian opened the oven to check on the lamb. She turned the heat down. James was still looking through the cupboard, lifting containers to see what was in them.

'What's their surname again?' he said.

'I was trying to remember it before, but I can't.'

'It's been too long now, we can't ask them.'

Lillian shrugged. The fan in the oven was loud.

'We don't have any chips and the biscuits are stale,' James said. 'But I probably don't have time to go out.'

'They'll be here soon.'

'Do you think we should avoid mentioning that they were broken into?'

'No, I don't think so.'

James folded the cupboard door closed and walked over to her and kissed her on the top of her head. Sometimes she forgot how tall he was.

Hannah and Franklin arrived exactly on time. They all greeted each other at the front door. James and Franklin shook hands and Hannah and Lillian hugged and kissed each other. They'd brought a bottle of wine with them. It was a cold night and they smiled in the doorway. They looked pale. Lillian imagined them as survivors of some kind of huge trauma, then had to remind herself that she didn't know them very well.

'Let me get you a drink,' Lillian said.

'Sounds good,' Franklin said.

'It's a good thing we didn't have to drive,' Hannah said. 'Remember when we went to Alice's? Frank got so drunk he couldn't drive. We had to catch a bus.'

'We waited for a cab,' Franklin explained. 'But it never showed, so we went to the bus stop instead.'

Hannah said, 'My God, I was plastered.'

'It wasn't that bad. The way Hannah goes on about it, it's like she had to lug me home on her back. She just doesn't like public transport, she's spoiled that way.'

'We've lived next door for years and this is the first time we've eaten together,' Hannah said. 'Isn't that funny?'

'It is,' James said.

Lillian smiled and walked into the kitchen with the bottle of wine, while Hannah and Franklin started to shrug out of their coats. The bottle was surprisingly cold. Lillian imagined them pulling it from their fridge at the very last second before heading over. She opened it and poured two glasses. She could hear James laughing in the living room. For a moment she felt like locking herself in the bathroom again and she stood still, waiting for the feeling to pass.

★

When she walked into the living room they were all sitting at the table. She handed them their drinks and then sat down next to James, who put his hand on her knee. He'd put the stereo on and turned the volume down so the music was barely audible.

'I hope you guys don't mind eating right away,' she said.

'I'm starving,' Franklin said.

'It smells wonderful,' Hannah said.

Lillian nodded thanks. James started talking about his work. He was a lawyer at a real estate firm. He wrote up contracts. Most of his anecdotes from work had a hint of the in-joke to them. Usually when he talked about work to Lillian he would finish, look at her face for a second, and then say, 'I guess maybe you had to be there.'

When he finished speaking both Hannah and Franklin smiled. Hannah lifted her glass and drank.

'So you guys were burgled?' James said.

'What an ordeal,' Franklin said. 'There were so many reports to fill in. I really hate doing paperwork.'

'I wouldn't be able to stand knowing that some stranger had been in my house,' Lillian said.

'I haven't had a good night's sleep since it happened,' Hannah said. 'I never used to dream much before all this happened.'

'You should see her, sometimes she'll sit bolt upright in bed. I swear when I try to calm her down she doesn't even recognise me half the time.'

'It's been very traumatic,' Hannah said.

'All I'm saying is that it's a good thing we don't have a gun in the house.'

Hannah smiled and made her hand into a gun and pointed it at Franklin's head.

'Do you see what I'm saying?' Franklin said. 'That right there is a kill shot.'

Lillian excused herself to the kitchen again, drank a glass of tap water, and then came back out into the living room with the potatoes. She went back to the kitchen and returned with the lamb and then did the same with the rice. She served everyone then sat down.

'This all looks so good,' Hannah said. 'Thank you so much.'

Towards the end of the meal, while their plates and glasses were almost empty but they were still eating and drinking intermittently, James said, 'Was much taken?'

'That's the thing,' Franklin said. 'They mostly just broke things.'

'And vandalised the place,' Hannah said.

'And vandalised the place, yeah. They spray-painted our bedroom wall, threw our clothes around and tore them. They threw all my shoes and a couple of suits into the bathtub and filled it with water. They were expensive shoes and they didn't even take them. What kind of a person does a thing like that?'

'A few things were stolen,' Hannah said.

Franklin looked at his wife and then down at the plate in front of him. He lifted his glass from the table and glanced into it.

'A few things were taken, yeah,' he said.

'Like what?' James said.

'Just a few small things,' Hannah said. 'Nothing really that valuable. Nothing that would really matter.'

'At least you two weren't home when it happened,' James said. 'So I suppose that's something we can be thankful for.'

Lillian half-expected him to raise his glass in a toast, but instead he tried to spear a single grain of rice on his plate with his fork. He missed and tried again and again. She looked away and attempted to unblock her ears by moving her jaw while still keeping her mouth closed.

James had lit candles, the flames of which bent and flickered now and then by some imperceptible breeze. The candles hadn't made it bright enough to see what they were eating, so James had turned on the lamp in the corner of the room, which shot a full moon of light straight up onto the ceiling.

'Would anyone like a coffee?' Lillian said, standing.

'I'll give you a hand,' Hannah said. 'It was such wonderful food.'

'It was no trouble,' Lillian said.

They cleared the plates from the table and took them back to the kitchen. Hannah put them on the counter and then looked around the room, her head tilted as if she was only interested in the highest shelves. The front door opened and closed. Lillian looked out the kitchen window, to the veranda. Franklin was handing James a cigarette, and then lit his own and offered the light to James, who leaned forward. There was a light above them, and then beyond that the streetlight in front of their house, and then just the darkness.

'Is Frank smoking?' Hannah said.

'Yeah,' Lillian said.

'He was going to quit, he does quit actually, but then he's so agitated for weeks. The smallest things set him off. I go around the house like I'm the intruder, trying not to disrupt anything. He'll die from stress before he dies of lung cancer.'

Lillian opened the coffee pot and started to fill it with water. Hannah was leaning against the kitchen bench, looking out towards the front veranda.

'His work's been hard?' Lillian said.

'Between you and me, I think Franklin's been having an affair.'

'What?' Lillian said. She paused and then felt like that wasn't enough. To make up for this she added, 'I'm so sorry.'

'It's okay,' Hannah said, keeping her voice quiet. 'I was shocked at first. In fact I felt physically ill. Of course I couldn't tell Franklin that. I had to pretend I had a stomach bug.'

'How did you find out?'

'I've suspected it for a while, but I'm pretty sure she's the one who broke into our house.'

Lillian looked out at the front veranda. James and Franklin were talking and she could hear the low murmur of their voices. James blew out a puff of cigarette smoke and it hovered above them.

'How do you know? Does Franklin think it was her?'

'I don't know. Pretty much all that was taken was some of our pictures, a few ornaments, some, but not all, of my jewellery, and Franklin's golf clubs. He loved those clubs too. It's hard to explain but it felt personal.'

Lillian spooned coffee into the pot, twisted it back together, then put it on the stove and lit the burner beneath it. She said, 'That sounds so awful.'

'And Franklin didn't mention it exactly, but whoever did it spray-painted *Screw yourself faggot* on our bedroom wall.'

Lillian nearly confessed, right there in the kitchen, that she'd been sleeping with someone else, but whenever she'd thought about leaving James, or even gone to the extent of packing things into a suitcase, she'd pictured James in the house without her, sitting on their sofa and staring blankly at the walls. James going around and staring at each empty room.

She'd been with Tim only a few days ago, and he'd told her about the last time he'd flown a plane, about ejecting from it and shooting straight up into the air while his jet had tumbled down to the earth below him. He'd told her how he parachuted down and it gave him time to reflect on things.

He'd said, 'I'm not sure if I crashed that plane on purpose.'

'I've been having the time of my life in this apartment,' Lillian had said.

Now she wasn't so sure it was true, but she wanted to say the word 'fucking' to Hannah. She was fucking someone else.

Instead she said nothing and they stood next to each other in the kitchen. Franklin and James came back inside and Lillian felt a slight touch of cold air. The coffee pot started to boil out up into the spout. Lillian put four cups on a tray, along with teaspoons, a bowl of sugar and a small white jug of milk. Hannah lifted the coffee pot.

'Ah hell,' she said. 'Who says I'm right about any of it anyway?'

'It could be nothing,' Lillian said.

They both walked into the living room and sat at the table. Lillian looked at Franklin closely, then realised she was staring and looked away. James sat close to her and smelled of cigarette smoke. While they all drank coffee and talked a little more she had trouble looking Franklin directly in the eye and she was relieved, ten minutes later, when he pushed his chair back and said that it was probably about time he and Hannah headed home.

Once their neighbours had left James started washing dishes again. Lillian felt like going to bed, but didn't want to leave him in the kitchen by himself. She sat up on the kitchen bench, which was less comfortable than she'd anticipated, but she still didn't slip back down onto the floor. James kept washing and stacked plates, with suds rolling off them, into the drying rack. Lillian looked at him as he worked. She thought, as she did regularly, that his last girlfriend hadn't loved him as much as he'd deserved.

'That went okay,' Lillian said.

'Yeah,' James said. 'They're good people. Are you feeling better?'

Lillian took a moment to consider how she felt and then the power went out. In the darkness she hesitated to move, and James didn't say anything for the longest time. She could hear water trickling from the sink into the drain. They'd needed a new plug for a while now. She thought about mentioning Tim to James right then, while she had the cover of darkness, and then she could easily slip away. She breathed in.

'Don't move,' James said, and she jumped in surprise because he was much closer to her than she thought. She could feel his breath on her now. 'Is there anything around you could burn yourself on?'

'No, of course not,' she said.

Her eyes slowly adjusted to the dark. She could make out James's dark shape in front of her. She felt his hand then, on her thigh. He leaned into her and she put her arm around him and held on tightly. Their mouths were on each other and then she heard the metallic chime of his belt buckle. Lillian lifted herself up to remove her jeans and underwear.

The whole thing lasted a little longer than a minute and afterwards they were both out of breath. James leaned into her and he smelled strongly of himself. He cleared his throat. The power was still off and they stayed together like that for a moment.

'Is it just us, or is it the whole street?' Lillian said eventually.

'It's just us,' James said. 'Everyone else on the street still has their lights on. I should go and check the fuse box.'

Lillian nodded and said, 'Okay.' She felt James move away and heard him pull his pants back on. She watched his shape leave the kitchen. She waited to hear him bump into something, but he quietly glided through the room. It surprised her that the only sound he made was when he opened the front door. She looked around herself, at the benches and the cupboards, which were no more than dark shapes in a dark room. She got down off the kitchen counter and stepped heavily, to keep her balance, when she pulled her pants back on.

She looked around herself. 'James?' she said. The room felt cold now. She waited for the lights to come back on.

Drowning man

We all watched the drowning man from the side of the lake. Someone said that one of us should swim out and save him, but we were apprehensive. The drowning man, in his panic, could pull us down with him. We all knew the drowning man but none of us really liked him and he had no desire to be liked. Did that still mean he deserved to drown? We discussed it among ourselves on the side of the lake.

Brom had an excellent idea for retrieving the body: we could all tie our boats together and then sink hooks into the water and trawl the bottom of the lake. The problem with this idea was that the drowning man was still drowning and not yet a drowned body ready to be recovered. We waited on the side of the lake.

I tell my students that we waited, but they seem neither impressed nor horrified. They yawn and draw pictures on their desks, which won't last. The drawings will be wiped away by the cleaning staff. I don't view it as a means of artistic expression; these are not Buddhists who destroy their artwork to show us the fleeting importance of the world. All the students in my class are just vandals.

I don't believe they hate me, it just seems that whatever it is they need to learn, I am not the one to teach them. It doesn't bother me much. My mind is elsewhere when I talk to them, or when I write on the blackboard in chalk. I can't stand the feeling of that, though, so I try to avoid it. There'll be lots of dictation and hand-outs until the faculty gives me a whiteboard and some felt pens.

I don't know how drowning feels, though it could hardly be pleasant. I was once pulled out into the ocean and for a second I panicked and felt the cool rush of water over my head and a knotting in my chest. I managed to swim out of danger, but for a while it was terrifying. I'd sat on the sand and coughed and above me the sky had been light grey and unmoving.

When we pulled the drowning man's body from the water we all stared down at him. He looked dead. His mouth was turned downwards in a horrible way. I thought that maybe I should say a few words, but nothing came to mind. Someone bent down on one knee, close to the drowning man, to see if he was still breathing. Satisfied that he was dead, they relieved him of his wristwatch. They held it to their ear to see if it was still ticking.

Water spills under the classroom door. I first notice it when I drop a stick of chalk on the ground and it lands in a puddle. When I pick it up it leaves behind a white cloud that holds the chalk's shape for a second before floating apart. I look at the water coming in from under the door. I sigh and tell everyone that perhaps going home would be the best idea.

'Should I call your parents?' I say.

'We are too old for that kind of thing,' my class says.

Outside there is too much water. It fills the car park and comes down the corridors in small waves, each no more than a golden line moving across the linoleum. I think it's strange because it isn't raining. The water seems to be rising gradually.

'Well, it looks like none of us are going anywhere,' I tell my students and they all groan together like a goddamned choir.

I knew the drowning man's wife; I was sleeping with her. I turned up at her house to tell her the bad news and also, maybe, to sleep with her. She was more upset than I'd expected, even though no one had really liked her husband, including her. Whenever we were together she would lie against me and complain about him, her head rising up and down on my chest as I breathed.

I was holding a bouquet of flowers. When I held them too close to my face, the smell made me a little light-headed. The drowning man's wife asked me if I had anything to do with it.

'What's that supposed to mean?' I said in my best hurt voice, but I could tell it wasn't enough.

In class my students call me 'Teach' or 'Teacher' or 'Sir', but never by my name, which is Richard. None of them has ever brought an apple to class and placed it on my desk. The other teachers in the staff lounge are well liked. Between classes they are usually eating apples.

Water falls from the ceiling. I tell my class that we need to get to higher ground, and they scrape their chairs across the floor and fill their backpacks with their notebooks and pens. Outside it begins to rain, but the flooding preceded it, I'm sure. I make a mental note of it because that kind of thing seems important.

I lead my students up the stairs, which has become a gentle stream, towards the roof. I tell them that the elevator, in this kind of situation, would be unsafe. It seems like the wrong idea, I know, to head towards the roof if water is cascading down from there, but my students need leadership and there isn't really anywhere else to go.

I once conducted a study on drowning. This was after the drowning man's wife had decided never to see me again. I went around with a tape recorder and interviewed people who had come close to drowning. I put an ad in the newspaper.

One man told me that after a near drowning he decided to join a popular religion. A lot of people, after they had almost drowned, had made life decisions of varying importance. The decisions ranged from asking people to marry them, to simply changing the carpet in their living room.

I wrote about how being that close to death makes you more decisive. Logically it wasn't that big a leap. I've never been the deepest of thinkers. Still, I did experiments on myself, in the bathtub with a brick on my chest, because I figured my life could do with some changes. I had water stuck in my ears for a week.

The drowning study was for a regional university. Afterwards people began to offer me teaching jobs, because of the success of the study.

The door to the roof is locked. I try to kick it down, but that sort of thing is much harder than it looks. My legs hurt and I have no other plan. I sit down on the stairs, water streaming gently past me. I prop up my head with my hands. I can feel the seat of my pants getting wet and it starts to become uncomfortable.

A lot of the students start to make jokes, mean jokes, about me. I can't hear the jokes specifically, but I can tell enough about them by the way the students are laughing and by the way they look at me. One student pats me on the shoulder in a possibly unkind way. I suppress the urge to cry, and tell them all to go back down to the classroom.

My drowning study won an award and for a while people were interested in it. It became a bit much. I got sick of being interviewed about drowning. I am well versed on many other subjects. I can pull apart a car engine and then put it back together. I used to be pretty good with a pottery wheel. I can whistle a tune almost to the note, though even I don't really see the value in this.

I spoke on a panel, to a half-filled auditorium. The other members of the panel were all experts on drowning. What a gloomy bunch. I slouched in my chair and didn't offer much. One man, who was bald and wore glasses, was the most outspoken of us. He said usually the people who drowned were the ones who had the least to live for. The others nodded in agreement. Ten minutes after the panel finished I called one of the universities from a public phone and accepted a teaching job.

In the classroom we wade through water that's waist deep. The desks have all floated together in a group to the east wall. I open the door outside and more water rushes in. It rises to just below our armpits and then continues to rise gradually. I tell my students to find anything that floats and leave the building. They stay still and I try to think of anything in the classroom that could be safely used as a flotation device. I tell the students to swim for it.

Outside the world is mostly water. Benches and fence posts and picnic tables float past. I tell my students to find something that floats and never let go. I'm thinking, Watch out for undercurrents, they can suck you down like a straw, but I figure my students don't need to be more worried than they are. This will have to be where we all go our separate ways. I tell my students it will all be okay, that if we can get through this then some big changes may be coming for all of us. I climb on top of a blackboard and manage to catch my breath. It's a relief to find that water is no longer filling my mouth.

Acknowledgments

Thank you Krissy Kneen, Kristina Olsson, Robyn Sheahan-Bright, John Hunter, Julia Stiles and Madonna Duffy, for helping this become a book.

And to Chris Currie, Fiona Stager, Benjamin Law, Kristina Schulz, Anthony Mullins, Bryan Whalen and Belinda Jeffery for their friendship and support, along with Angela Meyer, Favel Parrett, Ira McGuire, Chris Bowman, Alan Vaarwerk and Samantha Mee, for reading this collection in its very early stages.

To Ronnie Scott, Tom Doig, Ryan Paine, Katia Pase and Sam Cooney for helping me work on some of these stories over the years, and to Stuart Glover, Jason Nelson, Nigel Krauth and Steve Stockwell for their teaching and guidance.

Thanks to my mother, Adele Somerville, and my brother, Jack Somerville, and the rest of my family. Thanks to Bronte Coates for her love and support.

Add to your collection with UQP's short fiction series

THE REST IS WEIGHT
Jennifer Mills

'A writer of extraordinary range and imagination'
CATE KENNEDY

A girl searches for her lost grandmother while her parents quarrel at home. A young architect finds herself entangled by a strange commission. A man contemplates inertia after toxic fallout changes life in a remote Australian town. A woman imagines a mother's love for her autistic son.

The award-winning stories in *The Rest is Weight* Mills reflect Jennifer Mills' years in Central Australia, as well as her travels to Mexico, Russia and China. Sometimes dreamy and hypnotic, sometimes dark, comic and wry, Mills weaves themes of longing, alienation, delusion, resilience, and love. Collected or on their own, these stories are both a joy and a wonder to read.

'Shifting effortlessly from the naturalistic to the deeply surreal, these stories conjure a whole sensory universe and the exiles who inhabit it with images that lodge in your head and just won't leave. Mills' precision is breathtaking.' CATE KENNEDY

PRAISE FOR JENNIFER MILLS

'Clearly a talent' *Australian Book Review*
'Highly original' *Sydney Morning Herald*
'Brilliant' *Bookseller and Publisher*

ISBN 978 0 7022 4940 2

UQP

TARCUTTA WAKE
Josephine Rowe

'The stories in *Tarcutta Wake* are potent machines of emotion.'
WELLS TOWER, author of *Everything Ravaged, Everything Burned*

A mother moves north with her young children, who watch her and try to decipher her buried grief. Two photographers document a nation's guilt in pictures of its people's hands. An underground club in Western Australia plays jazz to nostalgic patrons dreaming of America's Deep South. A young woman struggles to define herself among the litter of objects an ex-lover has left behind.

In short vignettes and longer stories, Josephine Rowe explores the idea of things that are left behind: souvenirs, scars, and prejudice. Rowe captures everyday life in restrained poetic prose, merging themes of collective memory and guilt, permanence and impermanence, and inherited beliefs. These beautifully wrought, bittersweet stories announce the arrival of an exciting new talent in Australian fiction.

'The stories in *Tarcutta Wake* are miraculous for the human vastnesses they sound by the sparest and surest of means.'
WELLS TOWER

PRAISE FOR *TARCUTTA WAKE*

'Mysterious and satisfying' *Australian Book Review*
'Packs a punch well above its weight.' *Sydney Morning Herald*
'A wonderful talent' *Overland*

ISBN 9780 7022 4930 3

UQP